To Lexi,

A book is an adventure, so let it take you away! Your imagination is your gift to the world! Go beyond! Enjoy!

Love,

For my mother

And

For all those children writers out there,
Whether known to the world or known to themselves,
or not known to either

And also

For Kyla, because just as I shaped her, she shaped me.

Thank you.

www.mascotbooks.com

Beyond the Waterfall

For more information, please contact:
Mascot Books
560 Herndon Parkway #120
Herndon, VA 20170
info@mascotbooks.com

Library of Congress Control Number: 2016906966

CPSIA Code: PBANG0516A
ISBN-13: 978-1-63177-831-5

Printed in the United States

Beyond the
Waterfall

Eryn Flynn

PROLOGUE

Picture a world where the color blue is sacred, where everyone is born knowing how to swim, where water is everything. It exists...

Aquarius, our planet, lives up to its name. It's as strong as Titan himself and has mysterious legends about the past. Like the secret Clear Waterfall.

Legend has it that it never stops running, and over it, there's no water, just land. A person called the Waterkeeper looks after the waterfall, making sure it works properly. This waterfall is hidden – it has been for a thousand or more years, apparently, and no human has ever entered its grounds.

My name is Kyla Marine. I am daring, of average intelligence, and sneaky. I'm sixteen years old. When I was little, my mom never unlocked doors she didn't want me to enter. Still, I always found the key in her special drawer that I wasn't supposed to be able to reach, in a box hidden by shadows. But I quickly grew taller than her, and there was no hiding then. I took on a lot of traits from my mom – red hair, soft hands, but height was not one of them.

My best friend is Awanata Blue. We met in kindergarten and have been best friends ever since. She has blond hair with wisps, hazel eyes, and perfect freckles. Her mother left her and her father when she was about seven, but going through that only made her a better person. She's my soul-sister, and she gives me a lot of support and laughter. She tends to be better than me at most things, like smarts, being compassionate, and generally just following rules, but I've always beat her in athleticism.

Aquarius works a bit differently than Earth. We have roads, but very few and only in isolated areas. Our most common way to travel is in waterways with boats, or by paddleboard for teenagers like me. Boarding schools are the only kind of schools on our planet, and most schools span about five grades. To see their parents, kids schedule appointments with their parents' companies – that usually means vacation.

It's true that Aquarius is a lot different than Earth. Earth has stories and so do we, most of them being true. But sometimes I seriously wonder about what isn't.

CHAPTER I

On Friday, I had a bad start to the morning. Not only did I get to sleep late the night before, but I woke up late, too. Katrina, my roommate, was no help either, since she hogged the bathroom for twenty minutes. "Guys!" Myrtle, my other roommate, called from the door. "You comin'? We're gonna be late for first class!"

I had been trying to find a breakfast-to-go item, but was getting frustrated because all the cereal boxes in our little cupboard were empty. Flustered, I said to myself, "Huh! I'll just grab a...a granola bar or something!"

I grabbed my backpack and headed to the open door, Myrtle halfway through. "We're leaving, Katrina," Myrtle said and shut the door behind us. The sound of Katrina's blow dryer began to fade.

"I completely forgot about the time change. Did you?" Awanata asked me after first class, when we were walking to second class.

"Completely," I replied, sounding dull by the end of the word.

Awanata, knowing me very, very well, knew that that was partially a clue that I wasn't having the best day.

"Sorry," she said.

For a while we were silent, just walking with our books in our hands to second class. My mind began to drift to my stomach, which seemed to be begging for more food, since I had gone with just a cinnamon granola bar for breakfast.

All of a sudden my books went flying, my hair got loose and a skinny, short girl landed on top of me, with her books in my face. "Ouch!"

"Wow, just like, wow! Couldn't you see me coming? You've got to watch where you're going, like, seriously!" the girl said while climbing off me. At the first sight of her shrunken face, I recognized her as one of the most popular girls in the grade – Yuana Tidal.

In real life, she's a good head shorter than me. But her high heels add about two-and-a-half inches. Getting up myself, I noticed she had her gang with her. She outnumbered Awanata and me by two. Suddenly, she and her girls began giggling and pointing to me.

"What?" I asked Awanata through clenched teeth.

"Kyla, your hair is out!" Awanata replied in a loud whisper.

Oh, that's not good, I thought. My elastic was the only thing from preventing my hair from being a monster, since in the morning I was rushed and didn't get to brush it. Quickly spotting the bathroom, I ran through Morgan and Yuana (who were still laughing) to get to a mirror. Once I was there, I finger- brushed my hair after taking off my special bracelet. My bracelet had been my grandmother's, and on it was a charm of a moon with a face. I put my hair back into a neat bun and went out of the bathroom. Yuana and her pals had left. Only Awanata was there, waiting for me with my books in one hand and her books in the other.

"Thanks," I said.

Awanata gave me a face with one eyebrow up and one down. "Your bracelet?" she questioned. Without saying anything, I quickly turned on my heel and rushed back into the bathroom. I breathed a sigh of relief as I spotted it on the counter. With no time to spare until second class, I slipped it on.

I turned to the door, still looking at my hand. But I turned the corner too sharply and banged my knee against the wall.

"Ouch!" I shouted and held my knee, looking at the wall. Since I didn't have a very good temper and no one was around to see me, I smacked the wall with my hand in retaliation. "Owwwhat is that?!" I asked aloud.

I peered at the wall, moving my head to try to see it different ways. But after studying it from one angle, my jaw dropped. What I saw shocked me...a *handle*. But on a wall? And why that low?

I went on my knees to look at the front of the wall. But I couldn't see anything, so I decided to run my fingers along the wall. Just then, a knock came from the door. "I'm leaving, Kyla!" Awanata warned on the other side.

"Yeah, yeah, okay," I replied, not taking the time to process what she said.

My finger caught an indent in the wall. Squinting my eyes, I realized this crack had been painted over, making it nearly impossible to see. My hand followed this little indent horizontally until it suddenly turned vertically down at a right angle. Following it still, it turned horizontal again, another right angle near the bottom, and turned two more times before meeting back where I started. A little mystery stirred inside my head. In the end, the cracks formed the shape of a small square just the size so that I could fit in its area if I made a tight ball of myself.

Could it be drawers?

Could it be a vent?

Could it be a door leading to a secret passageway?

What was it?

CHAPTER II

"This spaghetti is more like disgustaghetti," Turtle, Awanata's friend, said. "I'm gonna go make my own. Hey, can I have your kitchen pass, Awanata?"

"First, the pass only works for dinner, and it's lunch. Second, you'd be late for your fifth class just waiting in that line alone, much less eating. Just go get some French fries," Awanata said. Turtle obviously didn't catch the tinge of annoyance in Awanata's voice, but I heard it, and smirked. Turtle would get on Awanata's nerves once in a while, and apparently had.

"Oh all right," Turtle whined despite a small smile while she got up to go to the line.

I looked around the cafeteria, with its high, high ceiling and its grand windows that took up the whole wall. We always sat at the exact same spot right next to a certain window. I looked at the single water droplets dripping down the window, then out to the dark sky. By the looks of it, we were going to have a storm.

I don't quite know why, but rainy days reminded me of thinking, and of course that day I thought of the "mysterious square." What if Awanata knew what it was? But before I could ask her, she started talking.

"Oh my gosh, I can like, feel my hair frizzing up! The weather has been way too humid lately," she said, looking out the window.

I laughed. Awanata was often teased about her frizzy hair by everyone. In fact, sometimes the science teacher would use her hair as a tool to predict the weather based on how wild it was. Her hair was usually pretty wild though, since it was so tropical in Dinta, where the school was located.

But back to the important topic, I thought.

Before thinking I said, "So, have you seen anything strange lately, like a small door or a hidden cupboard?"

Awanata gave me a *really?* look. "Tell me!" she replied with curious excitement.

After a moment's hesitation, I sighed and gave in. After all, it was Awanata. In my whole life I had never kept any secrets from her – not one.

"Well…" I started, but then stopped and looked around, making sure no one was listening. Leaning closer in, I said, "While I was in the bathroom I found something." Awanata leaned in closer, and her eyes got wider. For a second, she looked at me with expectation before I realized she wanted me to keep talking. "But you can't see it," I continued, which caused Awanata to be confused. "It can only be felt."

Awanata's face went from confused to majorly confused. "Like, in the soul or something? How'd you find it in the bathroom?" she asked.

"No, not in the soul! That's just weird! I mean I felt it with my hands," I said.

"In the bathroom?" she repeated.

"Not in that way, and eww! I felt it on the wall that

used to have that mirror. Behind where the mirror used to be," I stated.

"Uh-huh," Awanata said, giving some thought to that. She folded her arms and wasn't looking at me by now, but I could still tell she was listening. "So what was it?" she asked.

"Well, I found a handle on the wall and with my finger, I traced out the figure of a square," I said, motioning with my hand on the side of the table. "But the crack was painted over, so you couldn't see the shape."

Awanata turned back to me. "What do you think it was?"

"I dunno," I replied.

"Possibly a janitor's closet?" Awanata thought out loud, now turning her head to look out the window. A steady, grey drizzle had begun to fall.

"Mm, they already have a lot of other closets," I said, turning my head to the window as well.

"It just strikes me funny that they would have to disguise it," Awanata said. After a moment, she said, "Let's investigate."

I swear she was about to say something more, but then Turtle came back and interrupted our thoughts.

"Hey guys, guess what?" Turtle asked, carrying a big tray with a burger and fries.

We both turned to her, Awanata scooching over so Turtle could fit in the hard booth.

"Miss Shona, you know, the head cook, gave this water bottle to me for *free*! No charge whatsoever!" She exclaimed.

Awanata and I glanced at each other, our eyes letting each other know that the "investigation" from the previous topic was confirmed, and that we both thought that Turtle was overly excited. Throughout lunch, Awanata and I knew what the other was thinking, but knew to keep it a secret. The investigation had begun!

Over the next few weeks, Awanata and I both kept alert, looking for secret doors everywhere. We discovered doors in every corner of the Dinta school and city, each cunningly disguised. And, when Awanata went to a nearby city for an enrichment program, she found some there, too, on the city sidewalk once. That led me to one conclusion and one conclusion only – they were *everywhere*. In the town, in the city, in the Super-Continent.

CHAPTER III

"Hey Kyla, c'mere," Coach Rainier said.

I gingerly grabbed my element ball and walked over to him. Rainier is our Elements coach. Elements is a contact sport that is commonly played anywhere someone can afford to build a gym for it. It's similar to basketball, except the environment in the room changes randomly, from being a rainforest, to the Arctic, to anything in between. Right now it was on ice setting. The season's final practice had finished, so I didn't know why Coach had called me over.

"Try this," he said. Coach whipped the ice ball as hard as he could at the wall on an angle. It bounced off and hit me so hard I fell to the gym floor.

"You can only do that when the room's on ice setting. It's the only time when you can hit the opponent with the ball legally because it's indirect. You are the best player on this team, and I think it's time you should know it," said Coach. "Move your wrists like this and project the ball as hard as you can." I did what I was told, and within ten minutes I knew a new trick.

"Hey, thanks Coach. See you next season," I said. "Can I practice a few minutes more?"

"Sure, but turn off the lights when you leave," he said. "You had a good season, Kyla."

I practiced my shots a few minutes more. One of them

bounced off the rim really hard and hit the wall. The ball hit the wall so hard I thought it would leave a dent! As I moved closer to inspect, I realized that it did leave a dent. But not in the wall, in a *door*. One of those *secret* doors. And as soon as the ball hit that rusty old door, it creaked open. I stared in amazement. In that door was a dark, black tunnel. My mind began to stir. What did it lead to? Should I go see or should I not? But my curiosity won this battle. I knew I might curse myself later if I missed curfew, but I might thank myself too, if it paid off.

I put one foot in the tunnel. At first I was surprised at how low and small the tunnel was. I had to crawl to not bump my head. Then I remembered that the door must not close or I would be trapped, so I put my backpack against the door. Then, I was on my way. I was a little scared, but didn't admit it to myself. There were lots of twists and turns. After a while, the pathway gradually got narrower. It was so tight! Soon, I was on my stomach. It felt like blocks were being lowered on me. Finally, I just decided to catch my breath and think. So I stopped squirming, my stomach pressing against the cold, hard metal.

When is this tunnel going to end? What time is it? Is it past curfew? Thoughts ran through my head like fish in water. But, I decided that I had gone way too far to stop, so I kept going. Then, all of the sudden, the weight was lifted and I burst out of the tunnel. Within seconds I realized my location. I was in Palm Leaf City, the closest city to the school. That meant I was outside of school

grounds. *Let yourself enjoy this for a minute*, I thought before panicking. Palm Leaf was one of my favorite cities to go to. I let the cool breeze fly through my hair. I let myself wander a little, but not far from the tunnel opening. But then I laughed out loud. *Look at yourself, Ky. You know this place—this city, rather—by heart and you're not letting yourself have a little fun! You know the way to walk back to the school, even without a tunnel! Go have fun!*

That's exactly what I did. I didn't do much besides walk around, but there's nothing like walking in the bright lights of the city at night. While I was walking home though, something bumped into me, something very wet. I was on the sidewalk when it ran into me, and I fell into the waterway. Good thing no boats were coming! I looked up to see who had pushed me over. What I saw shocked me. It was a figure of a boy made up of water—pure water! His head was in the shape of a head, and his face was in the shape of a face, and everything else was in the shape it should be, but he was made entirely of water.

Whoa…was that just…the Waterkeeper!? I thought. The Waterkeeper was a character in a childhood myth that looks after the world. *Take it easy Ky, you must be really tired or dreaming or something! Just go back home and get your rest. Sleep in, because tomorrow is Saturday, okay?* I told myself.

I swam back to school grounds using the waterway. I was careful of boats, but none came. When I got back, I quickly snuck into the gym to get my backpack. I was so tired that I must not have noticed that the lights were off, despite the fact that they were on when I left.

"Kyla, wake up!"

Definitely not my best start to the weekend.

"Kyla, come on, get up! I know you're awake, so stop pretending to be asleep and get up!" Awanata shouted, shaking me back and forth in my bed.

"Huh?" I asked, sleepy-eyed.

"Ugh! Does this information help? It's 10:30! You've missed half the morning!"

At this, Awanata took a pillow from the foot of my bed and smacked my face with it.

"I'm up! I'm up!" I shouted and quickly sat up to show her. I rubbed my eyes.

"We're still going shopping today, right? At the mall? Don't tell me you forgot, Kyla" Awanata said, putting her hands on her hips.

I completely forgot. "What? No, of course not! How could I have forgotten?" My words were slurred because I was still so sleepy.

"Good. Meet me by the front doors as soon as you can."

I liked to tease Awanata when she sounded bossy like this, as if she was my older sister. So I said, "Ooh. Or what?"

"Do you really think this is the time to tease me when you just forgot and then lied about forgetting our plans to go shopping today?" Awanata hit me one more time with the pillow before leaving my dorm.

"Ugh," I groaned. Slowly, I shifted my weight to the edge of the bed. But I must have done it a bit too quickly. Down I fell to the ground. Good thing my thick pink rug was there. Also a good thing my nightstand was on the other side of the bed.

I got dressed and was out of the room by 10:45 a.m. I took the school tram – which was like a tram in the airport—to the front gates. I was very proud of myself. Even considering how sleepy I was, I arrived at the front doors before Awanata could annoy me for being late twice in a row.

CHAPTER IV

"Eeeek!" we both shouted.

"I can't believe it!" I squealed. "Are you seriously going next week too?"

"Seriously!" Awanata shrieked. We were both jumping up and down so hard that I was getting tired.

We were excited because my mother had just called to say that she had made plans for me to visit next weekend, which happened to be the weekend Awanata was visiting her dad in the same city! Once she heard, my mom had even made plans for us to stay in the same hotel! Now, Sunday night, we didn't have a lot of time to kill before bed and I wanted to make the most of it.

"How 'bout we celebrate on the patio? With some nachos?" I suggested. I would usually be uncomfortable inviting myself to someone else's patio, but Awanata was my best friend. She was like my sister and her dorm was like my second home.

Another thing: I love how our dorms were different. Awanata was on the first floor, so she got a bit of a smaller room, but in return, she got a patio and a bit of backyard. I however was on the fourth floor, so my room was a bit bigger, but I only had a balcony.

So anyway, Awanata and I had nachos on her patio until it was dark. We talked about what we would do on vacation. Before we knew it, it was time for me to go back to my room.

As soon as I shut the door behind me, I remembered that I'd forgotten to tell Awanata what I had done and seen the other night. But I kept thinking about it, and realized maybe I wasn't ready to tell her. This would be the first secret ever I didn't tell Awanata about. But perhaps it was a good thing that I'd forgotten. Like they say, everything happens for a reason…

"Are you ready?" Myrtle asked.

"No," I replied.

Myrtle led me down the hallway to Dr. Artic's office. Dr. Artic was the principal of Dinta's school. He was not very nice, to say the least. I was shaking so much I wondered if I'd make it to the end of the hall. I felt my heart pound against my chest and it became hard to breath. I was quaking so much that if I had a pencil in my fist, I probably would have dropped it.

Professor had called me in because he wanted to "calmly talk to me." Yeah, right. It was never good when a teacher asked for a student. I knew I was in trouble, but what for? I couldn't think of anything, except perhaps the tunnel. I wondered if Myrtle or anyone else knew about it.

I wondered if there was any way to get out of this. Perhaps I could pretend to get hurt. Or maybe I could pretend to get sick. I know how to pretend to get sick very believably. I taught myself how to when I was younger. That was when I hated school. No, that wouldn't work. At least not with Dr. Artic. *I'll get a penalty for that,* I thought. My assumption was that there was no way around this.

The red carpet hallway seemed to stretch as if it were never ending. I usually loved looking at the pictures on the walls of outdoor scenery, but all I let myself see now was the red carpet and my feet.

Usually my sneakers make a sound against the floor. But the carpet silenced them. No one else dared to say a word. *How can silence be so loud?*

"Kyla," Myrtle said suddenly. I jumped in surprise.

"We're here," she said.

"Oh, uh, okay." I was surprised my voice actually worked.

Myrtle began to turn the handle of the grand door. I think my facial expression must have given it away that I was scared because Myrtle said, "It's gonna be fine."

I looked into her eyes, which didn't quite meet mine, and saw a look of uncertainty. Something inside me didn't believe her. Instead, I believed I was entering Dr. Artic's hole and once you entered that hole, there was no way out.

I gulped and set foot in Professor's territory. *He's the predator and I'm the prey,* I thought.

I looked at the opening dark wooden door. It uncovered a darkly painted but well-lit room with hardwood floors and a red velvet rug leading to a desk. Dr. Artic's desk matched the door. On his desk were several teacher-related trinkets. One was a mug that said, "World's Best Principal." *Who gave that to him?* I wondered.

Without looking up, Dr. Artic said, "Come in Kyla, take a chair."

His voice echoed off the high walls and ceilings. A shiver ran down my spine.

Tentatively, I walked into the room, but my stride was more like a march because my muscles were so tight.

"You look like you have ants in your pants, juvenile. Just sit down." Professor looked at me over his glasses. He stared at me for a long second. Then I sat down in front of his desk.

"How are you, Kyla?" *Annoying, fake, professor-student conversation.*

"Good, thanks." There was an awkward silence, as I didn't carry the conversation. I wanted no petty chat with Artic. I wanted to get in and out as fast as possible.

"So, we all know nobody's perfect, but we also know that we must take lessons from our mistakes and possible consequences," Dr. Artic said.

Where is he going with this? I couldn't think of any rule I had broken lately. Well, not one that I thought he knew of...

"Kyla." He stopped. "As you know, there was some mishap at the gym Friday night, almost a week ago at the Elements practice. You were left with a responsibility Kyla, willingly. You know it is not safe to leave the gym lights on."

I waited for him to say something more, something about my leaving campus. But he didn't. *He doesn't know!* That was a relief. *I'd better roll with it,* I thought.

"Uh, yes I do," I said, sighing. "I forgot to turn the lights off. But I'll do better, I really will. I guess I was just tired. Yeah, I'll make sure to do it next time," I resolved, trying to sound finished so he might let me go.

"Even if that happens Kyla, you need to pay the price. You know very well that there is a thief on the loose. What if he had seen the lights? He would have known the school isn't on break. And what if he had found a way to get into the building? Kyla, that could have ended very badly," Dr. Artic whispered, getting faster and faster with his words.

My first reaction was to think that he hated me. It was stupid to say that leaving the lights on was dangerous— lights were on all over the school grounds. My second reaction I said aloud: "Wait – *what thief?*"

"You didn't hear?" Dr. Artic questioned, almost nervously.

I shook my head.

"Well, last Friday at the Shell Bank a thief broke in and stole more than 800 shells. He robbed a woman at gunpoint when she tried to stop him."

"Oh." The room seemed to get hotter. I wiped my sweaty palms off on my shorts.

"But anyway, back to what you're here for. You can't go around doing that, Miss Marine. Especially at a time like this. And in order to be fair to everyone else in the school, I must give you a punishment. And I have made up my mind – grocery duty," he said, his voice strong.

"What? Grocery duty? That's on Saturdays and it

takes up the whole day! And I'm visiting my mother this weekend!" I shouted.

"Mandatory," he said. "No buts. I guess you'll have to reschedule."

I rolled my eyes and sighed heavily.

"I'm sorry Kyla, but it's what has to be done."

I sighed, holding my head in my hands. I'd have to let Awanata down. "Who are my partners?"

"Myrtle, Morgan, and Dori are going to be your partners."

I suddenly sat up straight. "Wait, why Myrtle? She's like an angel. She never gets into trouble."

"Myrtle volunteered," Dr. Artic said in a matter-of-fact tone.

I sighed. *This stinks.* "Okay, lesson learned. Bye now." I said.

"Thank you for your time, Kyla. Have a nice day." I grabbed my bag and started out the door.

"Oh, and meet us at the bus stop," he called to me as I started to close the door. I walked away faster, leaving the door to slam. Grocery duty?

That night was a total disaster. Awanata cried. I felt so bad.

"Kyla, you (sniff) you knew I was looking forward to this weekend! Now I'll have to go without you (sniff)! I had so much stuff planned."

I felt so bad. What kind of friend was I? My eyes were

stuck to the floor of my room.

"I'm really sorry. I never meant for this to happen. I promise I'll make it up to you. I'm seriously sorry."

Awanata had a change of heart suddenly, even giggling a bit. "Just consider us even. I'm hoping now you won't be able to use the 'never-trip' against me," she said, the color coming back to her face.

We laughed, both remembering the never-trip, the trip that never happened because of Awanata's mistake. It had been a "weird" night where Awanata's morning class had been changed to a night class on the same day we were going to Sea Salt Island. Since it was so uncommon for her, Awanata forgot about the class. At dinner that night she decided to make a gourmet meal. But while making it, she heard the bell. She knew that meant that she had two minutes until class started. Not wanting to be tardy, she sprinted from her counter out of the kitchen, and *BAM!* Soup bowls went tumbling everywhere, the soup landing on Miss Shona and Awanata. Miss Shona had been carrying them when Awanata ran into her. To put things short, Awanata had to clean up, clean herself up, miss class, and be on table wiper duty for three days. Guess what she missed? Our flight!

Anyway, when I was done apologizing and Awanata was done crying, we headed to the cafeteria for dinner. I was glad my friend was feeling better, and so was I. We had fun later, too.

"Why is it that whenever we pass Mr. Marlin's classroom, he's always screaming at the class?" I asked Awanata on the way to the cafeteria. We both giggled. "No, serious-ly. I mean like every single time!" I said in between fits of laughter.

Awanata walked up to the wall of the classroom and listened in. "You are not *stupid*! You are capable of reading a paper about our country's history! So stop talking, grow up…" was the sound coming from the room.

"Okay, this is just gonna get ugly," Awanata said, laughing. "Let's just get to the cafeteria."

I wish I would have known to stop her.

CHAPTER V

"Hello girls! I saved your spot fir ya by the windows," Miss Shona, the head cook, said. As usual, she had a huge smile on her face. "It wasn't very hard, though. All the little kids are afraid to sit at an upper-classman table!"

"Oh, thank you very much! Man, even when you're as busy as this, you can multitask. Uh, congratulations by the way," I said, gesturing to her with my hand.

"Oh, why thank you," Miss Shona said. She blushed and looked at the tray of empty dirty dishes she was holding.

Miss Shona had actually won an award for "most interactive teacher" just a week before. She had given a big speech and received the trophy in the school's biggest auditorium, the room that feels as big as a city to me.

"Yeah, that was a huge win! I heard that was the first time in, like, twenty years that someone actually met the requirements for that award," Awanata said.

"Oh, thank you," Miss Shona repeated.

There was a pause.

"Hey, do you know what the weather's gonna be like tonight? It looks pretty wet right now, but what's later lookin' like?" Awanata asked, not really addressing Miss Shona or me in particular.

"Well, I heard it was going t' be a tee-storm, but I'm really not sure - my channel's always wrong," Miss Shona replied.

"It started raining around three o'clock didn't it?" I chimed in.

"Yeah, but I sure darn hope it stops," said Miss Shona. "I could really use a sunny day. Seems like we haven't had ourselves one fir a long time."

"Oh I know what you mean!" Awanata said, rolling her eyes at the inconsiderate weather.

Miss Shona gave a wistful sigh, as if breathing the last note of a song. "Well, you two better git a move on. Don't wanna miss those night classes!"

Awanata and I laughed and walked away. As soon as we arrived at the table, she put her over-the-shoulder book bag on her seat. Once I got there, I did the same.

"I think these should reserve our seats while we're up at the lines for dinner," suggested Awanata.

"Yeah, sounds good," I agreed.

While we were waiting in line, both of us talked and glanced at the little TV on the wall at the far side of the cafeteria. We both got a side of salad, chicken, and a choice of our own, then headed towards the desserts. *Pie...no...ice cream? Nah, not tonight. Oatmeal cookies? Yuck! Hey...brownies! Double fudge? Hey, that's Awanata's favorite! She'll be happy,* I thought. But then I frowned. I had accidently taken the last one.

"Uh-oh..." sighed Awanata.

"Here, you can have it, I don't really want it," I offered, not waiting for a reply before putting the plate of warm, gooey chocolate brownie goodness on her tray. Her face lit up with sincerity.

"Oh, thank you, Ky!" she cheered and hugged me as best she could with her tray still in her hand.

"Aw, it's all right." I had been looking forward to dessert, but I could sacrifice one brownie for Awanata. Especially after what had happened with grocery duty...

We got back to our seats and Awanata started eating and talking about the latest songs. I made a mental note that it seemed quite cold in the cafeteria.

Suddenly, Awanata stopped talking. The brownie fell from her hand and she shut her eyes tight. And just as suddenly as before, her face got red. *Really* red. Sweat quickly accumulated on her face in little beads. But wasn't it really cold in here? Awanata tried her best to cough.

"Awanata, are you okay?" I asked, trying to stay calm but not succeeding. Her hands flew to her neck and she shook her head no. I slid out of my seat to her and urged her to get up.

"*Help!*" I screamed, as loud as my lungs would go: "*Help! She's choking!*"

CHAPTER VI

Awanata's eyes rolled back in her head. She was frail and weak now, and I couldn't get her to stand on her own. But I knew we had to move...and *fast!*

I threw her arm around my neck and supported her waist with my free hand. In this posture, I could just about carry her, but she would still have to help herself walk a little bit.

I continued to scream. "Help! Please! Anybody! She's choking!"

This already drew attention to us fast. Some people just stood there, but a few called 911 for us.

"Miss Shona, someone's choking!" one kid said to her, pointing in our direction.

"My God...Awanata!" I read Miss Shona's lips to say. Immediately, she dropped everything she was holding and rushed to us. I tried to help Awanata move a bit to her.

Awanata's body felt like a crayon. I felt her body lighten bit by bit as I helped her to the sprinting Miss Shona. Her arm and body felt like they would break if I wasn't careful. Her face had reddened even more and she was still sweating a gallon a minute, but it was an unusual, cold sweat. But then why was her body so hot?

It took us only a dozen seconds to meet Miss Shona in the middle of the cafeteria, yet still, that was time we couldn't afford; time that was putting Awanata's life in jeopardy.

"Give 'er here, Ky," Miss Shona said in a panicked voice.

Miss Shona and I worked together to lie Awanata down on the ground. I heard Miss Shona mumble things to herself but I couldn't decipher them. She started to tap her pockets until she found what she was looking for and pulled it out of her pocket to reveal what it was: a flashlight pen.

"Open up," Miss Shona said, turning on the flashlight pen and pointing it down Awanata's throat.

More murmurs from Awanata and from Miss Shona.

I couldn't get myself to look at Awanata's mouth. I couldn't get myself to tear my eyes away from Awanata's shocked, hazel eyes.

I was completely unaware of the crowd around us but apparently they were too close to us.

"Back up! Back up!" Miss Shona shouted.

The crowd backed up a few feet. Suddenly, Miss Shona put away the pen and picked up Awanata's body, standing up and squeezing Awanata's stomach. She did this three times until something came out of Awanata's throat. Brown, gooey, and mushy, I realized it was part of the brownie Awanata had eaten.

Awanata fell – collapsed rather, out of Miss Shona's arms onto the floor, heaving on her knees. I bent down with her and put one of my hands on her back. Miss Shona bent over too.

A boy in green came over to Miss Shona and said, "Um,

I called the ambulance. They'll be here in any minute. And oh, they'll be arriving at door C."

Suddenly, as if in a movie, red and blue lights illuminated the south side of the room.

I suddenly looked up, not looking at anything in particular, and knew what I had to do.

Awanata was still struggling. Anyone who had eyes could see that.

"Now," I mumbled to myself. As I started to get up, I grabbed my best friend and carried her across me, like a baby, and ran. I ran through the crowd and through the cafeteria doors, and I knew the next door I would hit would be door C.

"Come on Blue, come on! Just a bit longer, I promise! You have to make it! You have to! I'm nothing without you Blue, *nothing!*" I cried to her, even though I knew she probably couldn't process what I was saying. While running with her in my arms, I found myself crying. But it didn't help.

It was all too much. Emotions in my head jumped around, afraid to hope but afraid not to. My best friend was scratching the face of death in my arms. And until she was in the hands of doctors, her life was up to me! Me! No one else!

"Come on, Awanata, please! You're strong! You're almost there! Please!" I cried. Finally, the lobby to door C came into sight and with it, the promise of help.

"Help! Please!" I shouted. People stared. I ran right past them to the ambulance outside, ready with a bed and nurses. Once outside they quickly spotted me.

"Help! Please! She was choking but I don't know why she's still struggling," I said to one of the doctors. They quickly pulled the bed out from the open-backed boat. The nurses and doctors said words like, "Hurry up," and "Move! Let's move!" to each other. Two nurses helped me lay Awanata down on the bed and hoist her up on the vehicle. Immediately, the medicines and tools came out to help Awanata.

I wanted to be right there with Awanata to hold her hand and guide her through this. I jumped aboard and hoped that they would let me stay on, but expected them not to. I was surprised when they shut the doors with me inside and started to drive.

"She's only partly conscious," the head doctor acknowledged. That didn't sound good... The third nurse, who was very short, started asking me questions about what happened. I got a call from Miss Shona saying she would meet us at the ER.

"How long hasn't she been conscious?" the nurse asked.

"I don't know," I replied. I didn't know anything in the corner of the ambulance there. All I knew was that I hoped Awanata was okay.

We had been lucky enough to get to the emergency room on time. Awanata had needed quite a bit of treatment to recover and was going to need to stay overnight.

Miss Shona had arrived with another professor – guess who...Dr. Artic! (Are you *kidding* me?!) She talked to the doctors and agreed she could stay overnight for health reasons.

I had just been listening to them in the waiting room and had been going in and out of the medical room to see Awanata. I had my ways of getting to know what I wanted to know. And I wanted to know what made Awanata so sick. By eavesdropping throughout the night, I learned that it really was the brownie. From nurse number three (who I started calling "Shortstop" in my mind), I learned that the brownie contained a deadly poison in it.

"But a normal brownie doesn't have that," I said to Shortstop.

"We don't know how or why," Shortstop replied, "but chances are that this was not accidental. And your school may be expecting the health inspector soon."

I sighed. "Okay, but could you please let me know how Awanata's doing?" I asked of her.

"Sure thing. Y'know, by the looks of it, you're a very supportive friend. I would've been glad to have you as a friend when I was your age," Shortstop replied, and walked away into the medical room. I was kind of glad she left, because my neck was getting sore from looking down. But I was so anxious to know about Awanata.

Although I pleaded, I couldn't stay overnight with Awanata, which I hadn't been happy about. But I had a morning class the next day and according to Dr. Artic, someone else's health was "no excuse" for me to miss class. Miss Shona drove me back to my dorm. It was hard to fall asleep that night because I was so frightened for Awanata. As I was falling asleep that night, a thought hit my mind: I almost ate that brownie.

Friday passed more slowly than a normal Friday. After all my classes I was given permission to take Miss Shona's boat out to the hospital to drive Awanata home. While in a main canal, the subject of the doors came up. I told Awanata about how I had gone into it, and where I had ended up. I told her everything—well, almost everything. I left out the part about that water-person because I still wasn't sure about it.

CHAPTER VII

Saturday wasn't very enjoyable. How can I be expected to smile when I have to get up early, do grocery duty, and get partnered up with Morgan to do it with? She's not quite the "thoughtful" type.

There was a rumor once that she threw stuff at her roommate a lot if she talked too loud or took too long in the bathroom. Myrtle was once roommates with her, and said that she took up the whole bathroom with her "pink stuff." And even I have experience on this one – if you're walking in the hall and you happen to be going at each other, she expects you to move, or else she's going to run you over and blame it on you. She is just like her best friend, Yuana, in that way. She talks about a lot of people behind their backs and is super-rich and self-centered. No one likes her very much, and I'm no exception.

I met everyone at the bus stop and found three cargo boats anchored at the side of the waterway. Cargo boats are boats with a small passenger space and a big trunk hooked on the boat's back. Dr. Artic split up the teams and bid us farewell. He had stayed true to his word: my team was Dori, Myrtle, Morgan, and me. But while in the store, Morgan was to be my partner – oh great!

Since Myrtle and Dori only had their permit and wouldn't be able to drive, they quickly went in the back seats. I started to the driver's seat but Morgan grabbed my shoulder.

"I'm driving," she said.

"But I kinda wanted to—"

"I'm driving," she interrupted me. "So move and let me sit in that seat!"

"Gosh," I mumbled while moving for her. "What a stingray."

We just slipped past each other.

"Excuse me?" she asked.

I barely made eye contact with her and turned away.

"Huh," she grunted and started the boat.

I felt the mood of the boat tense. Morgan drove us and then we parted. Immediately, things started out bad.

"I think we should start at this side of the store and work our way to the left," I suggested.

"No, it'll be quicker if we go by category. You know, like wheat to protein to fruit," Morgan replied.

"Whatever you say, Your Snobbiness," I mumbled. This time she didn't hear. I don't know how I managed, but finally we finished our duties.

We met the other groups at the bus stop. I really wanted to drive back to the school, since Morgan had driven earlier. I decided to see if patience would work with her, because I didn't know of any other tactic that did. It had been a long few hours with her. So I asked her calmly, "Hey Morgan. Since you drove before, do you think you could let me drive now?"

Her face contorted. "No, I wanna drive."

Suddenly I ditched the patience plan. "Come on, who says you're the boss?" She stuck up her nose at me and I started for the driver's seat. She protested and raced me for it, and when we met each other there, she pushed me aside—right into the waterway!

The boat behind us honked and came to a screeching, wavy stop. Myrtle screamed and the others gasped. Everyone came rushing to the sidewalk's edge.

In the water, I was so taken by surprise that I couldn't process the fact that I needed to swim. I would sink to the bottom of the waterway if I didn't act soon.

Suddenly, the water around me grabbed me, and tucked my arms and legs in. I was a straight, still line. It seemed that the water was hugging my back, and its "arms" were going across my stomach. The water seemed to almost swim for me. It "carried" me to the surface and thrust me onto the sidewalk!

Once I was on the sidewalk, the water dripped off me very quickly. In fact, quicker than the blink of an eye, but I glanced down very quickly, as soon as I could breathe – just in time to see two arms and a watery head retreat back into the waterway. Everything happened so quickly, so I didn't go after the water figure. Instead, I just tried to catch my breath.

Traffic was stopped in both lanes of the waterway. Boats were backed up going both ways. Myrtle and Dori had been holding their breath and let out a big sigh once they saw me, and both helped me out of the water. And as I got up, I shot Morgan the worst look she could imagine.

Her eyes widened with fear for just a second, and then she turned away. *This isn't the end of our rivalry Morgan,* I thought. *I'm going to get the last word!*

CHAPTER VIII

I thought about what happened later and it made no sense logically, but I understood it perfectly. Yet, I didn't *quite* understand. I decided that I was trying to think too fast and that I had too many distractions there in my room. Katrina and Myrtle were both back home for the night, and each was being quite loud. And I also saw that Katrina was "re-arranging" the bathroom so that she had a whole sink to herself and Myrtle and I would have to share the other.

"We have to take turns," she explained. "After all, there are only two sinks."

I'll worry about that later, I thought

"I'm going to the library," I announced. I needed to find a book on the Waterkeeper.

"Okay" Myrtle replied.

I grabbed my card and water board and went.

There was a mini one-person waterway that ran through the school grounds, which helped students get from place to place. With my water board, I rode in this waterway to get to the library.

I locked my water board to a fence and walked into the library. Once I found the librarian, I asked, "Um, hi, where can I find books on early water history?"

She escorted me to the west corner of the library. I thanked her, and then started desperately looking. I started scanning from one side of the shelf to the other.

"No...No...No...What?! Who even reads about that?" I thought aloud.

I scanned the whole shelf and found nothing. But at the bottom row of the shelf, the last book caught my eye. I pulled it out.

The book was dusty, and the binding was worn. The edges were fringed and the paper was yellow. As soon as I read the title, I was sure that this was the book I was looking for. The title was *Secrets of Aquarius*.

I sat down with the book at the most isolated table I could find. My hand got closer and closer to opening the book, but then I hesitated and decided to re-think everything over one more time before really doing "this."

I sighed and began to think. *Okay Ky, slow down. I paused. So I think I saw the Waterkeeper. I think he or she saved me. Did I maybe hit my head on the trunk?* I asked myself. I felt my head with my fingers—there were no weird bumps anywhere. I continued. *Was I hallucinating? No, 'cause I don't feel bad. In fact, I feel better than normal! But how? Ah, whatever...*

I thought for a while, but I found no explanation.

"Wow," I said softly, "I saw the Waterkeeper!"

That fact was hard to accept, because the Waterkeeper was just a character in childhood stories and myths. It was someone who was made-up, not supposed to be real. *But it is real,* I thought.

But why *me*? Why did I, out of everyone in the world, see the Waterkeeper, not once, but twice!?

I hesitated again, and then opened the book before I could stop myself.

The last time the world Aquarius saw its savior, the legendary Waterkeeper, was 3,864 years ago in the year 4012.

"Wow," I noted. "This book was written fifty-one years ago."

I continued reading. The book had more than a whole page about the definition of the Waterkeeper.

To the known world, the Waterkeeper has only been male in the past. There is only one Waterkeeper. A Waterkeeper's job is to look after the Clear Waterfall. As soon as a Waterkeeper-to-be turns thirteen, he becomes the Waterkeeper. A Waterkeeper can only be a descendant of the First One, the first Waterkeeper ever, and the first person to set foot on Aquarius. The majority of the world thinks that the Waterkeepers have always been secret. But before 3,864 years ago, the Waterkeeper lived among us, as us, with us.

I imagined walking down the street and running into the Waterkeeper like it was normal, greeting each other like old friends, because we are old friends. Way back, the Waterkeeper knew everyone and everyone knew him. There were no secrets.

I read on...

But then, the biggest disgrace our world has ever seen was born, and he wreaked havoc on our planet. His first name is unknown. We believe his last name was Hihc and we know he was male. Nothing else is known of this man.

Hihc grew jealous of the Waterkeeper, whom everyone loved. Hihc wanted to be just as famous as the Waterkeeper,

so Hihc did an evil act – he made a plan to get rid of the Waterkeeper, so he could take over.

He trapped the Waterkeeper and imprisoned him. If the Waterkeeper hadn't gotten out somehow, the world would've been doomed. But Hihc was caught and the people tied him on a ship and sent it off the edge of the world.

"Oh my gosh!" I said, becoming a little scared. "That means if his boat hit land in time, since Aquarius isn't really square, he could've lived and his descendants might be anywhere in the world!" I said, suddenly feeling unsafe.

After that, the Waterkeeper decided that there may be other evil people in the world, and that living among the people was unsafe for him and for the world. He disappeared soon after, leaving no trace of himself. Look for him, and you won't find him.

It is thought that the Waterkeeper may have some special way of transportation to get from place to place, perhaps invisibly or using super-speed. But there is no proof of this theory.

And then, in big letters at the bottom of the page it said, THIS IS ALL THAT IS KNOWN ABOUT THE WA-TERKEEPER.

I looked up from reading. I saw that some of the overhead lights of the library were beginning to turn off. I must not have heard them say they were closing, I thought.

Well, I needed to take this book with me so I could refer to it later. And maybe the rest of the book really wasn't about wars and had some other helpful information. A book this eerie and old probably wasn't even on the library record anymore, if it ever was, which meant I could steal it without being caught. Like a shadow, I crept out of the library with my book and headed to my dorm.

CHAPTER IX

When I got back to my dorm, all the lights were off. It was hard to find my way to the bedroom (my dorm had a bathroom, a bedroom we all shared, and another room that we used for pretty much everything else). The bedroom door was closed. As quietly as I could, I turned the cold knob and opened the door just a little and peeked in. Myrtle was sleeping in her bed by the closet wall, which was normal, and Katrina was sleeping in her bed near the other wall in a very awkward position on her belly, also normal. Everything in the room was normal - except for one thing: my bed, the bed near the window, was empty.

"And it'll stay empty," I said quietly to myself. For I had decided right then and there that I would try to find another secret door that night, and I would see where that one would lead me!

Soundlessly, I put my stuff down and crept out of the room. I decided I should try for the study hall - it was the easiest place to get to since it was connected to the dorms, and in the same building. I was slightly panting by the time I reached it.

The lighting was very poor. The only light in the room, in fact, came from street lamps outside. After looking for a good amount of time, I gave up on it that night, deciding it was too late and too dark to try to pull this off. I started heading down the hallway to the stairs. But as I turned the corner, I ran into someone – Dr. Artic!

For a minute he just stared and I took a step back in surprise.

Finally he opened his mouth and said, "And what would a girl of good, free birth like yourself be doing wandering the dormitory grounds at this time of night, Miss Marine?"

"I...I had to go to the bathroom," I stuttered, trying to think up a story quickly.

"And you couldn't use the one in your room because...?" he asked, gesturing for me to finish the sentence.

"The...one in our room broke," I lied. "Overflowed actually..."

He tilted his head, crossed his arms, and sighed. "Miss Marine, if I were not smart, I would not be one of the top professors of this school. I am smart enough to realize that you are not telling me the truth."

I opened my mouth to speak but Dr. Artic put a finger up and said, "Ah, but don't say you can explain, because you are just going to lie to me again when you do."

Wow, I thought. *How did he know I was gonna do that?*

"I've been working here for almost twenty years, Miss Marine, and I know the usual answers."

That would be how, I thought.

"I'm not going to force the answer out of you, Kyla," he started.

Finally, my first name! I thought.

"I will instead spare you a little mercy. We can keep this just between you and me," he said, "and I will not give you a punishment for roaming around after curfew."

I was happy he was "sparing me mercy," but I didn't know why.

Suddenly his face became less friendly. Not like it was friendly in the first place.

"But not everything is fun and games. You must go back up to your dorm right now, and that is a command!" he ordered.

"Thank you Professor," I whispered humbly, and started very quickly down the hall.

"...And I will know if you don't, Kyla!" He yelled to me from down the hall. "Good night!" he finished and walked away.

I went back up to my dorm with no hesitation. *That was too close for comfort!* As I fell asleep, I wondered why Artic had let me go with no punishment. He'd said he only wanted this between him and me. The only explanation I could think of for his actions was that he wasn't supposed to be roaming either...

CHAPTER X

The next morning was a beautiful morning! The sun was shining and there was not a cloud in the sky. I would've been glad to wake up to that, except for one thing. This is how I woke up....

"AHHHHH! I have a *zit*!"

Don't you just *love* the sound of Katrina's screaming voice? I don't.

I opened one tired eye and glanced in the trash. A pizza box.

Well Katrina, that's what happens when you smear pizza grease all over your chin.

"Myrtle, come and look at this!"

What is up with my weekend wake-ups lately?

Since I knew I wasn't going to fall back asleep anytime soon, I got dressed and got up.

When I walked into the main room, I could see Katrina in the bathroom using some exotic acne treatment and Myrtle was in a casual dress and a house robe doing homework.

Now looking at the floor, I understood why I had been tripping over things last night – there was everything on the floor from couch pillows to study books. I opened the curtains to the bay window in the room. Since the sun went right through their thin material, it didn't make much of a difference, but still.

"Mornin' sleepyhead," Myrtle greeted me.

"Morning," I replied, not fully sincere.

"Why did you come back so late last night?" Myrtle questioned.

"I didn't," I lied.

"Yes, you did," Myrtle corrected me. "Katrina and I fell asleep just a bit after curfew and you weren't back."

"Oh, come on, it was Saturday night!"

Myrtle stared at me, and then went back to looking at her books.

"Nice pants," she said, still studying. "I think that's the third day in a row you've worn them."

I looked down at my jeans. "Well, I mean, it's not like pants get dirty as easily as shirts," I told her. "Plus, it looks good with my shirt." My shirt was a *Palm Leaf City Rock Band* shirt.

"Yeah sure, it looks good..." Myrtle said, not trying to hide her sarcasm.

"Like you know fashion!" I said.

Myrtle pretended not to hear me because she didn't have a comeback for that one.

I glanced at the clock – 10:15 a.m.

"I'll be back by eleven o'clock," I said to both of them. I planned to take the weekly newspaper and read/doodle on it in the study hall. I would usually do it with Awanata, but she had just managed to get to Pure Sand City to see her dad. She had been determined not to miss the trip, even though she had just gotten out of the hospital. Honestly, I was still surprised she had been allowed to go, much less able to.

"Eleven a.m. or eleven p.m.?" Myrtle asked, teasing me about last night.

"A.m., smart-one," I snapped.

I opened the door, grabbed the newspaper, and went on my way.

The study hall was much brighter now than it was last night. The one wall was only windows looking out to the green outside. The study hall was on a corner of one of the dorm buildings. The hallways allowed you to either go west or north. The ceiling was vaulted.

I sat in a chair with a coffee table next to it in the corner, near the window wall. I clicked on my pen to draw a mustache on some black-and-white picture, but then I stopped. The headline caught my eye.

"Invention – Intention?"

What could that mean? I read the article. It was about a man who had just died last week. In his lifetime, he had been to prison three times. He was not a good man. When the authorities went into his house after they found out he was dead, they found a red laser pointer. They measured its temperature – 500 degrees Fahrenheit.

I stopped reading to look at the picture. The picture I had almost doodled on was a picture of him going to jail for the third time. The picture beside that one was a picture of the laser. Its height and width seemed slightly more than a pen's, which seemed small for such a powerful tool.

I continued reading. They ended up even finding documents suggesting the man was going to make thousands of these lasers, put together a team, and evaporate large bodies of water.

The authorities planned to blow the laser up along with any more they found. (They didn't find any more besides that one.) But when they went to do so, the laser was gone!

I gasped. *Oh no! What if someone else tries to evaporate water with it?! What if someone else learns how to make more?! The world could be doomed!!* I kept reading to find out where they found it stolen. They had planned to blow it up by Fish Tail Shore, but had kept it in Dinta before then.

No, no, no, it can't be! I thought, becoming scared.

I only had to read a sentence more to find out...yes! The laser had disappeared in Dinta. It was scary to think that I was sitting in Dinta at that moment. Authorities were evacuating the city of Dinta, but the newspaper said that they didn't plan to evacuate suburbs or schools yet. However, they were going to ask them to make curfew at 9:00 p.m. instead of 10:00 p.m. so that they could keep better track of the students. Also, they had asked schools to double the security inside and at the edge of the grounds. The rest of the article was just a reward for turning the laser in. I looked up from reading. Almost everyone in the room was reading the newspaper. After reading the article I wasn't quite in the doodle-and-make-fun-of mood. I grabbed the newspaper and went back to the dorm.

When I got there, Myrtle rushed to hug me. *Wow, I*

thought, *she went from teasing me to hugging me within a half-hour.*

"Oh Kyla, did you hear?" Myrtle shrieked, meeting me at the door.

"About the laser thing? Yeah, it was all over the newspaper," I replied, looking and sounding concerned.

Myrtle let go of me. "It was all over the news too! How horrible right?" she said, talking faster than normal.

"Yeah," I answered.

I walked into the room and Katrina was watching the news to learn more about it.

"Hi Kyla," she said.

"Hi," I said in return.

I walked over to the window. Now it wasn't bright and sunny. It was gray and cloudy, but no rain. *Perfect to match the mood,* I thought. I went back to thinking about the newspaper. Why would that guy want to put the world in jeopardy? Why would he want to evaporate water? And why would someone else steal the laser and want to do the same thing? All those people in the inner-city of Dinta could have been and still could be in danger. The school could be too, since we weren't far away. I tried to imagine being one of those people being evacuated, leaving my home for who knows how long!

How terrible! I thought. I was glad they weren't evacuating the school yet.

The rest of us were pretty silent for the rest of the day. I didn't go out or do anything.

CHAPTER XI

The next day was Monday.

Nobody likes Monday.

Not even the teachers.

It was a very long day; the morning seemed like the whole day and the afternoon seemed like another day. At lunch and dinner I really only played with my food. I was still in a weird mood. It didn't help that Awanata wasn't back yet. The evacuation of Dinta had postponed her flight until Tuesday. I wouldn't see her until Tuesday evening.

The week may have started out slow, but that was all about to change.

Awanata arrived back at school late Tuesday evening and after she was done unpacking, she came up to my room for a quick hello.

On Wednesday I had a lot of free time, so I took out the Waterkeeper book and thought about it at the library during lunch before my next class, which wasn't for another two hours. I wondered if I would ever see the Waterkeeper again. Probably not, but I promised myself to keep an eye out for him. Why did he save me? What if I saw him again? I thought about the answer to that question a lot but finally came up with one conclusion:

If I were to see him again, I would follow him. He had gotten away from me twice. He wasn't going to again.

Thursday passed and Friday came. On Friday I only had thirty minutes for lunch, but that was enough time to discuss the doors with Awanata. I sat with her at our usual spot.

"Y'know, I thought it was strange, but if I looked super-duper carefully, like, really, really carefully, I found doors in Pure Sand City," said Awanata between bites of salad.

"In what kind of places?" I questioned curiously.

"Well, like, oh...there was one door under my hotel bed! I accidentally dropped my shoe under the bed one morning, so I was trying to find it when my fingers came across the ridge of a door edge. I could barely reach it with my fingers. I literally had to climb under the bed! There was one that surprised me even more though. I found it impossible at the time, but..." Awanata stopped.

"Yeah...go ahead," I urged.

Awanata looked around to see if anyone was listening, and then she said, "I found one in the elevator wall."

My jaw dropped. "But wouldn't it be dangerous to use the door when the elevator's high up?" I asked.

"Well maybe we're just assuming too quickly. They might use it as, like, a chute for towels or something, and then pick 'em up at ground level," proposed Awanata.

"Yeah, but don't they have carts for that?" I asked.

Awanata sighed. "True…"

There was a pause.

I looked at the clock. Fifteen minutes remained before my next class.

"Well, I forgot a book in my room and I need to get it before next class. See ya later, Frizz," I said to Awanata.

"So…I'll catch up with you later?" Awanata asked.

"Yeah, sure, just call my room number," I replied.

"Okay, bye," she said.

I grabbed my bag and started toward door C, recalling the event that had just taken place a week before. I was very glad Awanata was feeling better. Then, thinking back to the door conversation, I sighed. *Well,* I said to myself, *that's the third Friday in a row that the doors remain a mystery.*

When I walked outside, the air was chilly.

Quite chilly.

I decided that while I was in my room getting that Waterkeeper book, I would grab a sweater too.

Right outside of door C, there's a waterway cul-de-sac that leads to another waterway – the main one that runs in the school grounds for a little bit and then out towards Dinta. I decided that I would take this waterway on the sidewalk to that one-person waterway to get to my dorm.

Once I was finally on the sidewalk, I waited to cross the street.

If I looked way up ahead I could see security boats parked on either side of the street looking in everyone's trunk before they exited the school grounds. It was extra heavily packed, thanks to the double security ordered after the laser crisis.

I was waiting patiently, humming to myself, when suddenly in the water right in front of me a human's foot made out of water splashed me! I had seen it clearly, and I had been well prepared. Every part of me knew that what I had just witnessed was the Waterkeeper, swimming in the water—as water—escaping security, escaping the world and everything around him. Escaping everyone – but me.

"Hey, hey, hey!" I yelled, getting louder and faster with every word.

Panting quickly and heart beating loudly out of pure adrenaline, I started sprinting along the sidewalk, watching him and making sure not to lose him.

Once I caught sight of him (now I was certain it was a boy), it was quite difficult not to lose him. All of the water around him was swirling rapidly and in every which way, confusing me. It was nearly impossible to see him, but somehow, I managed. I was nervous and determined to follow him. Not long after I started running towards security, two young boys were approaching with water boards in their hands.

I thought quickly. Even though it wasn't the right thing to do, it was what had to be done.

While I was passing them, I grabbed a water board right out of the hands of one.

"Hey!" he yelled in a strong voice.

"Sorry," I yelled back sincerely, but I knew he didn't

believe me. I could sense that he was starting to chase me.

I jumped into the water right in front of a boat, not losing sight of the Waterkeeper. Honks filled the air.

Oh no! I thought. We were coming up to security. I took a sharp breath in and then let it out, knowing what I was going to do. Nothing was going to stop me.

There was a small opening between the two lanes.

As quickly and aimfully as a dart, I shot through them. More honks and yells.

I knew I was crossing the legal line at that point. But it didn't matter. The Waterkeeper was within reach. I mean, how many times does that happen!?

"Hey!" one of the security men yelled. "She must be the laser thief! Arrest her!"

CHAPTER XII

After security, I had a bad feeling about going through like that. But if I had done it legally, I would've had no chance at following the Waterkeeper.

I quickly looked back twice after cutting security. There was a lot of commotion and I worried they would chase me. It took them a few seconds longer than I thought it would, but eventually they did. *Don't panic*, I told myself. *Just keep your eye on the Waterkeeper.*

The road was empty after security. I sped up and moved toward the middle of the waterway. Now the Waterkeeper was right in front of me.

I was panting so fast I thought I wasn't breathing at all. My hands broke out into a cold sweat. In the distance the police were chasing me. And within two feet, the Waterkeeper was swimming away from me. But I wasn't going to let him get away.

Not this time.

Inside I was screaming, but outside I was silent. It was weird to think that at that very second, a lot of people thought that I was a criminal. The whole world was on edge, fearful of the laser, that they would desperately take anyone as a suspect. And if they caught me, I would be treated like a criminal.

What if they did catch me? What would I do? What would Mother and Awanata think once they saw my face plastered on newspapers and TV screens with the headline: CRIMINAL FOUND! LASER – MISSING! What would they do??

Suddenly, the Waterkeeper moved. It startled me so much that I let out a squeal and lost my balance, and nearly fell off my water board! It took effort, but by wildly waving my arms, I recuperated my balance and sharply came to a stop.

The Waterkeeper stopped suddenly and jumped onto the sidewalk and across the grass, "dripping" to the left and away from the street. I jumped off the water board and onto the sidewalk. Even though I was tired, there was no turning back now. Relentless, I kept chasing him.

"Hey!" I yelled, "Stop! You're not gonna get away now!"

I ran really hard, lunging for him, but always missing. From doing so, I was covered in mud nearly from head to toe. My threats and commands eventually turned into pleas. I didn't think it was possible to be that tired, until I was.

"Please," I begged, "Pu-leez?"

We came to a corner and I stumbled to my feet. Just as I fell, giving up, I saw the water spring up, into that form of a boy again. But it was hopeless. Now I was lightheaded and dehydrated, a very dangerous health condition, and tired out of my mind. But as I fell, I could see the Water-keeper make another turn up ahead.

But did that matter?

Day was ending. Even though I was in the forest, I could see the sky through the trees.

Why had I come this far, only to fail again?

It seemed as though the world was falling apart. The world was in danger because of a laser. The Waterkeeper kept revealing himself. School seemed not to matter. And worst of all, this had to all stay confined in my mind, unable to be released, building up pressure like cotton in my ears.

I watched the pink, merciful sky turn to a majestic black playground for the Children of the Stars.

While feeling the leaves and soil on the ground get cooler, a little bit of comfort came upon me, remembering the story of the Children of the Stars.

Grandmother used to tell it to me. She used to be the best storyteller for miles around. She used to tell it to me by the fireplace in her best Scottish accent, with me on her knee. It went a little something like this:

"One day, Queen Luna (better known as the Moon), went to a party. Sun was there, Water was there, and even Soil was there to celebrate. Queen Luna had just a bit too much fun, and stole one of Sun's rays. With it, she set the whole world on fire.

She was punished, thrown into the sky and banned from Earth. Her punishment was that every night for the rest of forever, she had to polish the stars. But Queen Luna was much too selfish to take this punishment, so she gave birth to the Children of the Stars and made them polish the stars.

Sun, who was the King, thought this was unfair, so he changed this as much as possible. So before a child must polish the stars, he or she has a chance to be free in a time period called Life. After Life is over, the children must polish the stars.

Someday I will polish the stars and someday you will too. But do not be afraid, because polishing the stars is a wonderful chore that makes the Children very happy. Moon will forever be blinded by her own vanity, while others who aren't will laugh and polish with joy."

Looking up at the sky, right there and then I knew Grandmother was polishing a star. Just at that moment, it looked like the star I was staring at somehow got just a bit brighter...

CHAPTER XIII

My eyes bolted open.

The sun was shining on my face through the trees and I was looking up to a clear blue sky. I sat up and looked around briefly. I was at the part of the woods where I had lost the Waterkeeper. *I must find the Waterkeeper*, I thought.

Turning to the direction I needed to travel, I started to get up.

"Hey, hold up!" a low voice said, a firm hand grasping my wrist and pulling me towards the ground.

I turned to see a boy a little bit older than me with dark hair and dark, gentle eyes in a soft face, reaching out a long and graceful, yet strong arm.

"What?" I whispered, only loud enough for my ears to hear.

"Come on! Give your body a break!" he said to me, receding his hand.

I didn't say anything, but my face undoubtedly showed my confusion.

The boy leaned back and laughed a jolly laugh while holding his stomach.

"Sorry about that. Name's Determine, but you can call me Deter."

I stared.

"This morning I saw you in the woods and I could tell

you were dehydrated by the way you were breathing, so I stopped. Dang, you've been sleepin' a long time, 'cause it's 2:00 p.m.! Uh, Saturday," he said to me.

I still didn't say anything.

"Uh," he said while reaching into his bag beside him. "Here, drink this."

He held out a bottle of water.

Gratefully, I accepted.

After two gulps the water turned sour, and I shivered.

Deter laughed his jolly laugh again and then said "It's medicine water. It'll help you get better really fast, but I know it tastes bad. Hey, keep drinkin'."

"Thank you," I said when I finished and handed him the bottle. "I'm...actually feeling better already." I had become aware of a terrible headache the moment after seeing the boy Deter, but now it was fading.

"Ah, no problem. Hey, so I've told you my name and how I found you, so you tell me your name and how you got here."

"Uh," I hesitated, "My name is Kyla."

"How'd you get here?" he asked.

"Uh, I...can't quite...remember," I replied. I couldn't just tell him about the Waterkeeper.

"Ah, that happens when ya get dehydrated," he said.

He mumbled something I couldn't make out.

"What?" I asked.

"Ah, nothin'. So...you feelin' better?" he questioned.

"Uh, yeah. How long did I sleep, by the way, and where are we?" I asked.

"You actually slept eighteen hours I think. And welcome to Dry Cove."

"Pardon?" I asked him.

"Dry Cove," he said. "If you look all around, way out in the distance you can see a little hill..."

Sure enough, all around me, way out in the distance was a big green hill.

"...It kind of makes this land a bowl. About 500 years ago, this area was underwater by a darn good amount," he said.

"Cool," I said, looking around.

"Hey," Deter interrupted the silence, "are you hungry at all?"

I concentrated on my stomach.

"Surprisingly, I'm starving. Like, I'm famished!" I said.

We both laughed. Deter helped me up and we stared down the road. But before we went, I etched the letter K into one of the trees so I could return to that spot to find the Waterkeeper.

"Do you like breakfast for lunch?" he asked.

"Absolutely!" I replied.

"Cool! I know the perfect place!" Deter announced.

For that moment, I felt like I could mend my sores and get back on track. Maybe I would discover the Waterkeeper stuff, and return to normal life. For that moment, while Deter and I were heading on our way, I felt as though everything was going to be all right. For the first time in a long time, I felt good.

"Here, the restaurant's just around the corner," Deter said. "We're almost there."

Deter turned out to be a very kind, funny boy. He also knew the area very well. He was very tall, and his voice was so low that it seemed to vibrate in the air sometimes.

"Ya know Kyla, it's a little bit strange that you have no one and nothing with you, and you live in – where did you say? Dinta? That's half a day's journey away. Why was no one with you, like a friend or parent?" Deter asked.

"Well, my mother lives in Pure Sand City and I don't get to see her much," I said.

"Father? Sibling?" Deter prompted.

"Um...well...," I hesitated.

"Yeah..." Deter urged. I could tell he was curious.

I sighed. "My dad was barely ever around. Now I'm talking about, like twice a year for half a week maximum. And it got to the point that my mother got tired of it. Supposedly, he had some job in the government and it would be illegal to tell my mother about it. So you could say that I never really met him because that's somewhat true. I had a brother, and surprisingly he was close to my dad. I don't know how though. But one day my brother went with my dad and we never heard from them again. My mom doesn't ever talk about it. But she said once that my brother was only four. I trust, though, that they're in a better place," I said.

I was surprised at myself. That was the first time in many years that I had shared that scar. The last time I talked about that was to Awanata in the third grade.

Deter was silent.

I tried to think of how to change the subject.

"I'm sixteen—how old are you?" I asked.

"Ah, well, by the sound of it, I'm as old as your brother would be. Eighteen. But don't tell anybody – I'm *serious*."

"What? Why?" I asked.

"Ah" Deter paused. "Well first of all, I don't have any siblings. My mother died four years ago of a sickness that was popular in the area. It was a sickness similar to yours, so that's why..."

"...That's why you came and helped me," I finished.

"Yeah," he continued. "And then my dad was just kinda mean. I didn't like him one bit. I'm glad he's gone. He just died recently. But anyway, it's illegal to live alone under the age of twenty-two, so I lie and say I'm twenty-two because I look it. I wouldn't be able to go to school because I can't afford it. And since eighteen is too old to be in an orphanage, the government would put me in jail since I'm legally homeless. But so anyway, I have a job and I know these woods pretty well. Everything's good. I don't mean to get down or anything. I'm doing well enough and I trust that my mom's actually in a better place, polishing the stars," he said.

"What?" I asked, astonished.

"Ah, it's just a story," Deter replied.

"I know that story too! My grandmother told it to me. I trust that she and my dad and brother are there too," I said.

"Hey, cool! I always liked that story," Deter said.

"Me too," I added

"Hey, hold up," Deter interrupted. "It appears as though we're here."

We had a nice lunch in a little bistro and talked. It was as if we had known each other for a long time. After lunch, we just walked around the city. I noticed that the city of Dry Cove had roads instead of waterways, which was surprising. Water seemed to cost a lot too.

"Hey, why does it seem that water isn't as common here?" I asked Deter.

"Ah, well, this area is pretty dry. It's virtually a desert compared to the rest of the Super-Continent. It's one of the five driest places. Now, that doesn't mean that the area's parched, but pretty close to it," he responded. "It's part of the whole 'dry cove' and 'dust bowl' thing."

"Oh, I see."

"Yeah," he said, "Water sure does empty your wallet here!"

We both laughed. "I believe it!" I said. I felt a little bad for him, because the way he had just laughed seemed to signify that he struggled with the price of water. I tried to imagine what it would be like to have to work so hard just for vital necessities.

We started into the woods to his house, which he told me was more like a hut of earth, leaves, and sticks. One thing confused me about our conversation though; why did the Waterkeeper pass through one of the five driest places on Aquarius? *Well,* I thought, before entering the woods, *hopefully I'll find out soon enough.* Deter's house, once we got there, was rather impressive.

"This isn't a hut!" I told Deter. "It's more like a clever-ly-made cottage!"

The little house had walls of tightly packed dirt (and a coating of clay) with a stick skeleton. The roof, being only about four feet off the ground, was flat, also with a skeleton of sticks and leaves woven into it. It looked like it could fit about four people.

"I wish that were true. I can only sit or lie down in it and there's not much room anyway," he said.

I replied, "But still. Usually it's only you and your backpack, so does it matter? Seriously Deter! This is really good!"

Deter grinned sheepishly. "Thanks."

After a quick tour of his "lot," Deter asked me if I could fetch firewood and he would start the fire and make dinner, which was some soup we had brought back from town. We soon got the fire going and I thanked Deter for sharing his food and everything else with me. I would have been still sick without him! It was also extremely nice of him to let me sleep the night, since I had nowhere else to go.

"Ah, no biggie," Deter said when I thanked him. "I usually don't have any company and it's nice to have a companion and not be lonely for once. Well, not lonely at my house anyway."

During dinner (which was quite tasty), we talked a lot about every subject. We exchanged stories back and forth and I found it quite intriguing. Even though I hadn't known Deter for very long, I felt like I knew a lot about him. One of the conversations that was brought up was Deter's house.

"Um, if the area is so super-duper dry, then how did you find clay? It's only in very wet soils isn't it?" I questioned my host.

Deter looked around and then said, "Ah well, I can't say that I know. It's suspicious to me too. But one day, I was just walking ya know, and I tripped on a hole! A hole! It was a perfect circle, about the size of my and your body widths combined, and I decided to look closer. It went down for what seemed like a long time. And the sides of the hole were pure clay! How 'bout that?! Pure clay! So I took, well, a lot of clay and built my house with it. The hole widened quite a bit, but whatever."

"But I kept it a complete secret," Deter continued, "because I know that clay would go fast here. So whenever I'm done taking clay, I cover up the hole with leaves. That way, it remains a secret and in my possession."

Waterkeeper, anyone? I thought, but only replied, "Wow!"

"Do you wanna come see it?" Deter invited.

"Yeah, sure! But don't worry, I'll keep it a secret," I assured him.

"Thanks. Let's go!" he said. Deter gestured for me to come.

I suspected that the Waterkeeper had something to do with the hole, so it didn't surprise me when Deter took the path that I had seen the Waterkeeper taking before I lost him the day before. As we turned left, I made another

"K" in a tree to mark the path we were taking. We went not much further before Deter moved some leaves on the ground to reveal a hole as wide around as the thickest tree trunk.

"Wow!" I marveled. "This is astounding!"

"Thanks. I think it's really cool," Deter responded.

"Oh yeah! Totally is!" I agreed.

Deter showed me the hole in more detail. Indeed, it brought forth very pure clay. We stayed until the sky was dark, and made little figures of each other out of clay, which triggered a lot of laughter. When we got back to the hut, we put out the fire and prepared to sleep. I felt that the day had been good, and sleep sounded good too. Before dozing off, I decided I would search the hole further, and possibly even go inside it. What if the Waterkeeper went into it every day? That would explain the clay too.

Yes, I decided. *I am going to search that hole as soon as morning arrives.*

CHAPTER XIV

The glow of dawn awakened me. Far off in the distance, I could see an orange-silver glow at the east side of the land bowl. There was barely enough light to see anything at all though. I could not see Deter clearly, even though he was just a few feet away.

Rising, I walked over to the figures of clay that Deter and I had made the day before. I took the one he had made of me, wrapped it in a leaf, and carefully placed it in my pocket. It meant a lot to me and I couldn't bear to leave it. I then walked over to Deter.

"Thank you," I whispered.

The sun was rising quickly now and I had no time to spare if I wanted to get to the clay hole secretly. I was walking away toward the horizon and the hole as I took one last look at Deter's camp. Then, one last look at Deter.

What if I never see him again, I thought. For the most fleeting moment, I wondered if Deter was my brother.... But the moment passed just as quickly as it had come.

I had to get going. I walked for a little ways before I saw that first K carved in a tree. Walking along that path was not easy – it was hard to see in the dim morning light and roots and rocks came up frequently in the ground. I must have stubbed my toe a dozen times.

Suddenly, there was a dip, and my left foot sunk into something. For the first second, I was frightened, but then I realized I had stepped in the hole.

I got out and stood back. The hole was right there. *Now is my chance,* I thought…*Right now.*

The daylight was a little bit lighter, but not by much. *Um, well, maybe I should just turn back,* I thought. I started to turn, but stopped midway. *No – I have to go.* I turned around again. *Should I go or should I maybe just turn back? Yeah, I should turn back. But NO!* I was at war with myself.

I got to my knees and leaned over the hole, letting my hands support me, grabbing the rim of the hole. It went deep. Really deep. So deep that everything just became black. *Am I really thinking of going in there?! I am crazy! What on earth could possible happen if I hopped in there besides stupidity? But how come there's clay here anyway?* I thought. *This could be a once in a lifetime – once in the world's history – chance of finding the Waterkeeper.* I looked in the hole again. It looked scary. My heart was beating faster now and my hands were starting to sweat. I could hear my thoughts screaming at each other in my head. It got louder and louder and became overwhelming. My head started to thump and I swallowed and took a deep breath. The thoughts were still screaming.

All of a sudden, everything became silent. The screaming thoughts stopped and the birds were silenced. As I looked in again, the hole seemed even blacker. The color was so intense that it had an emotion with it. It was a blinding black. Even with little imagination, it looked like the four corners of Nothing in the whole Universe all connected right there.

I listened again. It was still silent. The hole was still black. I didn't have time to think anymore. I couldn't think.

And then, as fast as lightening, I dove head-first into the hole.

CHAPTER XV

Now I felt that everything around me was slimy – the clay – but packed very tightly. I was unable to move my body even an inch.

All of a sudden, for some reason, I became terrified; more scared than I have ever felt in my life. The fright was unbearable, and I didn't know what to do. Shaking, heart pounding, and scared for dear life, I cried. And the fear didn't go away. I cannot explain my fright in words.

I do not know how I breathed, for there was clay all around me, but somehow I lived. Possibly it was the moisture in the clay or something else. I cried and quaked and prayed until I fell asleep –I actually don't know what happened, but I blacked out– in the hole, aimlessly hoping for, well, I don't know what.

The hole was quite mysterious, for after I fell asleep, somehow I awoke lying on the ground with forest around me. For a moment I thought it was the same forest I fainted in, but quickly I realized that it wasn't. This was a greener forest – the other one was a bit more barren and brown – and this one was glorious indeed! I looked around. I didn't see the hole anywhere, just a mossy forest floor. I didn't recognize anything about my surroundings – it was all so strange and beautiful.

But how did I –

Oh, I guess I won't be able to figure it out, will I? I looked around again. In front of me was a stone wall, great in size. Green vines were growing on and through it. I stood up. It was a rugged wall and very rough, yet sturdy, tall, and intimidating.

Why is it here? I thought. *And what's behind it?*

I touched the middle rock and pushed on it. To my surprise it moved! It retreated into the wall and the whole wall, more than three times as tall as me, separated down the middle.

Wow! I thought. *This is amazing!* The wall revealed a dark alley, also made of stone and vines. I was so excited that fear did not strike me at all. Running with excitement, I started into the alley.

Everything was very natural along the wide path. I loved the greenery – it was a very vibrant green everywhere. The alley was slightly curved to the left. It lasted for a little while, but I was not able to estimate a certain distance in measurement of any sort. When the path was nearing its end, everything became brighter, a green more beautiful than any color of green I had ever seen. Yet I was not able to see what lay ahead because the alley curved and there was a curtain of a weeping willow tree. I stopped right before the wall ended and where I would be able to see the landscape ahead. Excitement built up inside of me. I hesitated, but stepped forward and drew the willow curtain back. There in front of me, was a scene that was unlike anything in any world, dream or imagination!

I listened for a minute. There were beautiful bird songs and a breeze was rustling all of the leaves around to make a calming, natural sound. The green color was magnificently vibrant. All parts of the ground were covered with a blanket of grass this color.

There was a large pool in the center of the big clearing. Feeding it was a great Waterfall, bigger than the dorm building in Dinta itself! It was massive and I could feel the vibrations in the ground caused by the great pounding of the water. The sound was smooth and quite powerful. All of the water rushed into the pool. Over to my right, there was a little creek being fed from it, which grew bigger as it meandered lazily along, and then curved out of sight. The bridge to this creek was made of moss.

The color of the water – oh the glory! It was purer than Awanata's pure soul, purer than the blue icebergs of Alaska, purer than the flawless sky and blazing sun, as if it challenged the gods themselves!

Surrounding the majestic paradise was a forest of its own glory. There were weeping willows all around the area. They were beautiful, and the ones near the lakebed's leaf branches cascaded to the water so that the last few leaves floated on the water's surface. The breeze made them sway over so gracefully. There was also a little island by the Waterfall before the creek separated it from the mainland that I was now standing on that had beautiful birds that sang and luscious grass and weeping willows that swayed in the breeze ever so gracefully.

Looking all of this over, I became overwhelmed. Everything that had gone on earlier had made it seem as though my life was falling apart, and now, I come to see this! How lucky, how blessed was I to have everything I had. The sight stirred me. Was I really appreciating everything I had? My family, friends, possessions? I had a renewed, thankful spirit watching the Waterfall.

People were not made to take in this sort of paradise – that was my conclusion. Queen Luna must not have made man capable of taking in such a heavenly sight because I couldn't comprehend this.

My throat tightened, my eyes closed, and I cried. I covered my face with my hands and bent down on my knees on the cloud-textured grass. It was unbelievable. And there, with my tears falling into the water, hands covering my face, knees bent, I – Kyla Marine – cried because I simply was not made to comprehend such paradise and I didn't know what else to do.

After I cried, I felt different. It was as if I had to pay my shame and then I was forgiven and renewed. So, after crying, I rejoiced.

I ran, laughing, through the beautiful willow trees, and the sound of my laugh and the rustling leaves combined to make the sound of chiming bells. After running a ways, I dropped on the grass and laughed some more, looking at the weeping willow leaves stretching toward me and I lifted up my arms and reached toward them. The grass was softer than the whitest cloud on Aquarius. It was softer than Grandmother's heart or a king's finest piece of silk. I rolled around and around in the grass and ran everywhere. I embraced the place.

What stirred me most was the Waterfall. It was magnificent and intimidating and I trembled before it. Looking from the grass, curiosity of the pool suddenly won, and without thinking, I took a running start and dove into the water. The temperature was perfect—not too hot, not too cold, and very refreshing. There was something extraterrestrial about this water, because it was just too magical. I swam for a while. I don't know how to describe the feelings, for they too, were extraterrestrial. But I recognized a little confusion in those feelings – what was this place? What was beyond the Waterfall? Would I ever find out?

Well, for now, I would just have to wonder. I had to go back to Dinta, but I vowed I would return. And soon...

CHAPTER XVI

It was clear as glass that I couldn't go through Dinta the normal way. Security would put me in shackles, falsely accusing me as the laser thief. The world was so desperate now to find the thief that they were willing to charge any suspect whatsoever. Thinking of a way to get back, I knew it wasn't going to be easy returning, but going through the hard way would just have to do.

I had to go through dense nature and sneak into the school grounds disguised. Although, I doubted it would work. But on the other hand, it was the only chance I had at all. So, I would just have to try.

It pained my heart to leave the paradise, but even so, I got ready to leave. I wrapped the statue that Deter had made for me in one of those sacred leaves. When I was ready, I pushed on the middle of the great stone wall, and it separated once again.

The next challenge was getting out of that forest. I searched from evening to night for the hole without any luck. I had no choice but to pick a direction and keep walking in it. It was generally dark that night, so the only light and beacon or compass that guided me was Grandmother's polished star. I walked for a long time, but I don't know quite how long or how far. There was just something so majestically eerie about that forest.

By now, it was very late. I decided to try to sleep.

Hopefully, in the morning I would be able to find my way back to Dinta so I could arrive for Monday classes. But of course, I had no idea what would really happen.

The morning was surprising. As unreal as it seemed, I woke up in the forest outside of Dinta!

I had to delay my curiosity though, because I had to hurry up for class. Sneaking in quietly, I soon arrived at the main square. It was bustling like a busy city. The campus clock that towered over the square read 8:45 a.m. My language arts class would end at 9:00 a.m., so I had practically missed it. My next class started at 9:10 a.m. so I had twenty-five minutes to get ready and report my "vacation" to the main desk. I would have to lie and say I went on a last-minute trip to my mother's for the weekend and my boat arrived late. When I reported it, the lady at the main desk was very suspicious, and even though she marked me down, I could sense she didn't believe me. Not one bit. But at least I got passed.

Next, I went to my dorm. I was the only one there. I threw my clothes in the laundry because I had been wearing them for three whole days, and they were gross! I quickly showered, cleaned up, and got ready for my next class, which was science. Then off I went.

I arrived at class four minutes early and got my things together. The room started filling up very quickly. Some people had just gotten out of theology class, so they were buzzing about the religion they had learned about. By overhearing their conversations, I learned that this religion was the oldest known religion. It had the Sun and

Luna involved, even the Waterkeeper, and it sounded like the religion that the Children of the Stars were from. I didn't tend to think of myself as religious. My father's side of the family had believed in Luna though, so I did, I guessed. Grandmother had told me all about her when I was younger. I believed in Luna and that Grandmother was polishing the stars, but I had never thought deeply about them before, or thought about what my believing in them meant. Mother hadn't really adopted the whole religion after the disappearing incident that Father had pulled. I decided to keep quiet and not say, "Hey, that's my religion!" because this religion was illegal, untrue, and lots more, according to the talking students. They said it had no followers anymore...

It was hard to concentrate on science after listening in, but I managed. The diagram on the board was about the moon's phases and ocean tides.

"Now, you have all heard about the crazy Luna religion, right?" Professor asked.

The religion they were talking about, my religion! There was a hum of "yes" from everyone but me.

"Well," Professor continued, "this religion was almost completely based on the moon."

We talked about the moon's phases and the magnetic force the moon has. I learned that high tides are closest to the moon and directly opposite, and low tides occur everywhere in between. Neap tides and spring tides were also discussed.

The rest of the day I couldn't stop thinking about

the theology students' conversation. It was hard to concentrate.

At dinner, Dr. Artic approached me. Nostrils flaring and glasses almost falling off, he addressed me unpleasantly.

"Miss Marine, you missed grocery duty last Saturday!" he growled.

I was taken by surprise but thought of a way out. "Last time I was almost severely injured, sir. I thought it would be unnecessary for me to attend again. I meant to contact you, but I had to urgently rush to my mother's. I am very sorry, sir."

"What emergency brought you to your mother's so quickly?" he asked, even though it sounded like a statement.

"Private family troubles, sir." I said it with attitude, accenting "private" and "sir."

"Very well," he said with hesitation. "You may have table wiping duty instead. But since I am merciful it will be for this meal only." And with that, the turned on his heel and went.

"Sheesh. What was that all about?" Awanata asked from across the table.

"Nothing. I really don't give a thought," I replied.

Awanata shrugged. I loathed the job but I washed the tables after dinner, knowing I was actually lucky that only this much discipline was enforced on me. Once I was finally done, I went to my dorm. As fast as I could, I did my homework and chores and washed up for bed. Myrtle was cleaning up the room and Katrina was watching a movie. But I was so ready for sleep that I just crawled into bed and looked out the window that was near my head. The room was dark, so I could see very clearly outside.

Lying there in bed, I began to wonder about science class again. Why was my religion illegal? Did my believing in it make me illegal? What would happen to me if people found out what I believed in? I knew that I would have to be very secretive and not let anyone find out that I followed Luna's Way. I would just have to pray for safety. I became scared, but for some reason more determined too, to follow Luna's Way.

"Keep me safe, Luna," I whispered to the crescent moon. Then I dozed off into a dreamless sleep.

One thing struck me before dozing off – Deter followed Luna's Way too.

CHAPTER XVII

The rest of the week passed awfully slowly! Classes seemed to get longer and longer and free time shorter and shorter. I was just dying to get out again. When the weekend finally arrived, I decided I would go to the waterfall again – but this time legally, without cutting security.

I rented a boat for the weekend as soon as school got out on Friday. I would be able to use it for three days – Friday through Sunday. At my dorm, I unloaded my school stuff and packed some snacks and water bottles, as well as a few clothes. Then I took all of those supplies and put them into the boat. When I was ready, I took off.

It was a small boat, but it was all I could afford. It was for two people and had a small trunk. It had a hood and was low to the water, so low that if I opened my window and put my arm out, I could feel the cool water of the waterway. Since I had left right after school, I beat most of the traffic, but not all of it. Traffic was somewhat backed up near security, but I passed through smoothly. I had feared that I wouldn't, but the man who checked my vehicle was dull and not very alert, so he barely even questioned me.

After that, it was a breeze. I drove as close as I could to Dry Cove. I parked the boat and paid enough to park it there for the whole weekend. Then, grabbing my things, I headed to the woods. The "K" I had carved in the trees led me right to the hole.

My eyes started to water with fear again, but nonetheless I jumped into the darkness.

This time I knew what to do. I woke up after being transported through the hole. Once again, I could remember nothing but darkness.

When I awoke, I appreciated the greenery again and approached the great stone wall. Pushing the middle stone, I felt a thrill when the walls separated, exposing the paradise to me once again.

I thought I would have been over it, but still the beauty paralyzed me. The birds, the water, the grass, the trees. Oh, the purity and joy! It felt as if whenever I went there I became a new person – not my usual self, but someone who truly felt love and gratitude through and through. In fact, I spent the whole late afternoon walking around admiring the place.

Next were necessities. I put together a hammock out of weeping willow leaves to be my bed for the next few days. I had a few snacks from my bag, which I set down near my new bed.

One thing that I remembered from science was that Aquarius' moon goes through a full cycle in a bit more than a week. It wasn't a full moon tonight, but one stage away. It would be a full moon on Sunday.

I lay in my hammock, looking at the stars in the sky. Suddenly, the glitter of the mostly full moon on the water caught my eye. I looked at the reflection some more. It became hypnotizing. Robotically, I walked to the edge. The water was almost glowing. Still hypnotized, I dove into the water – straight into the moon's reflection. The water was perfect, even at night. Even though I had never thought of jumping into the pool, I felt like I had wanted to my whole life and now I was satisfied.

Morning brought new light upon my face. I woke up by the sun's warmth on my cheek.

I had gotten used to the beautiful sound of the splashing waterfall. I walked to the land's edge. The waterfall was only feet away now. The mist dampened my face. The waterfall's powerful pounding penetrated the ground and my feet. Looking at the magnificent cascading water, a strange and familiar feeling returned.

Oh no, I thought. The hypnotism again…

Instincts immediately took control. I was scared and confused, but there was nothing I could do. I leaned towards the waterfall so that I was inches away. With no time to get back in my right mind, I moved my hands to the waterfall. Magically, I separated the waterfall as if it were a curtain!

I gasped. *Is this what lies beyond the waterfall?* I looked into another world all its own. This world had diamond, crystal, and water. Astounded, I walked inside. The water curtains closed behind me ever so gracefully. It made the place darker, but I could still see.

The first step I took was pleasing to my bare feet. I

looked down to see that I was walking on a cloud! In fact, the wide hall was completely carpeted with this cloud. In the stone walls there were ancient texts, but I was not able to read them.

At the end of the hallway, there was a small pool. It was a beautiful, perfectly clear blue. On the wall there was a small shelf with nothing on it, and above it, a plaque that read, "3,915." There was a decoration on the stone wall above this: an intricately carved moon. But this moon was different than most moons. This one had a face.

I raced back to my hammock, darting through the waterfall and speeding to my bag. I tore through it, searching for only one thing: the book that I had stolen from the library, *Secrets of Aquarius*.

"This must be the place of the Waterkeeper!" I said to myself. "For sure. The hole led me here and the Waterkeeper led me to the hole. The Waterkeeper is in touch with Luna. The carving is Luna. And since Luna's Way is illegal, his home is the only place where a Luna carving would exist. This paradise is the place of the Clear Waterfall, which the Waterkeeper takes care of. It makes perfect sense. And this is another puzzle piece…"

I opened the book.

The last time the world Aquarius saw its savior, the legendary Waterkeeper, was 3,864 years ago from the year 4012.

"That's it! It's in the first sentence!" I said. I did the math. It added up. 3,864 + 51 = 3,915. I cheered, bouncing up and down with the book in my hand. "I figured it out! I'm at the Clear Waterfall! I know what's beyond the waterfall!"

All I needed now...was the Waterkeeper.

CHAPTER XVIII

Trying to catch the Waterkeeper wouldn't be easy. I knew it wouldn't be; Waterkeepers have a tendency to be elusive. But I had to seek him out. I hid my things and hid behind the bush by the waterfall entrance, waiting for him to arrive.

I waited a while, but there was nothing. Finally, the stone wall entrance opened! The figure of a boy made of water, the Waterkeeper, came running out.

"Hey!" I yelled, and threw the stone that was ready in my hand. I didn't mean to hurt him, I meant to get his attention.

He dodged the stone, looking at it go past him and then looking at the rock's origin - me. When he saw me, he looked for his usual escape - water. He ran and dove in the water. I did too. I knew it was dangerous, but I did it anyway.

He's going for the entrance to the waterfall, I thought. I planted myself right under the falls' front step. When a wave of water hit me, I knew it was him. I held on to what was probably his shin and tried to hold him back. He couldn't go much further.

Yes! I've got him now! I thought. I pulled and pulled and soon I could see we were near the shore. Then I thrust him with all my might onto the shore. I popped up and quickly pulled myself onto the dry land too.

The water boy coughed. Then, for the first time ever, he turned into a real person! I gasped. The Waterkeeper, in human form, had flowy blonde hair, light freckles, and beautiful blue eyes. He was a little bit taller than me, and very muscular.

I barely allowed him time to get to his feet. "Who are you?" I snapped, using a strong and confident voice.

"Look, what do you want? I'll give you anything," the Waterkeeper replied, putting his hands to his chest.

I paused. "What?"

"Look, just tell me whatcha want and get out," he said.

"I am not here for riches," I stated. "I'm here for *you*," I said, gesturing to him with my head and taking a step forward.

"What?" he asked, taking a step back. He seemed a little scared.

"Tell me who you are." Of course I knew who he was, I had already figured it out, but I wanted to know more—I wanted to know every secret about him and this place.

The boy hesitated and let out a huff. He scanned me over and said, "You must tell me who you are first, in order to get anywhere with me." He smiled a devious smile.

I squinted my eyes at him, popped my hip, crossed my arms, and sighed. "I'm Kyla Marine, daughter of Thetis Marine, a student at Dinta, sixteen years of age and wondering who *you* are."

He laughed. "I already know who you are. And you know who I am."

There was a pause. I was shocked. *How does he know who I am?*

"How do you know me?" I asked, out of breath. He just smiled knowingly, smugly. "Tell me!"

"You're not going to get what you want if you keep yelling at me." I hated his annoying smirk, telling me he knew he had the position of power.

I'll find out how he knows me later, I thought. I said "Fine. I do know who you are. The Waterkeeper. This is the third time I've seen you."

"You're pretty good," he said. "Which times are you referring to?"

"Once, you pushed me off the sidewalk into the waterway. The next time, I was sinking in a waterway and you saved me. And then now," I finished.

"Why'd you ask me who I am, if you already know all that?" he questioned.

"Because I want to know more," I answered.

"What do you wanna know?"

"Everything."

"You don't want riches?"

"Why would I want riches?"

"You're strange," he answered.

"How many times do I have to ask?" I was quickly becoming flustered.

He sighed and seemed to be contemplating something. "I guess I don't see the risk in it. You have no reason to tell. Come with me."

I obeyed with no hesitation. It seemed to me that the Waterkeeper was very stubborn and hard to work with. *Maybe the strategy of wrestling him and sweating it out of him would have worked better,* I thought. Nonetheless, he led me to a different part of the waterfall—the far edge.

"Here," he said, and opened the waterfall like a curtain just as I had. What I saw astounded me.

It was the inside of a grand house. The ceiling was higher than usual and there was a fountain in the middle. The carpet was again as soft as a cloud. It was all one big room with dim, natural lighting, but perhaps my eyes just hadn't adjusted yet. In the corner there was a cloud-like waterbed. In another, a homey little kitchen, and in another, a living room. Some rooms or areas were divided by glass walls with waterfalls running silently down them. Even though the place seemed magnificent, it still felt cozy, warm, and homey.

"Wow," I gasped. "This is wondrous."

"Thanks," he said, "C'mere." He turned the corner and we came to a little room. This ceiling was low and the walls were covered with blue tiles. There were eight pews, four on each side and three aisles: two small ones on the sides and one bigger one down the middle. Once again, water ran down the walls into the rocks that bordered the room. There was a different carving of a moon on the wall and a table in front of all the pews. Looking at it, I knew it was a small chapel.

"Look, it's, uh, it's Luna," the boy said to me.

It was hard to take all of this in. In just a day I had done so much…

"What does all of this mean?" I asked.

"This is a temple. What do you mean, what does it mean?" he replied.

I sat in a pew.

"Well – I don't know, what does the moon mean? What does this place mean? What does the waterfall mean? What does everything mean?" I pondered aloud.

The boy paused, then said, "Well, first of all, I saw that you had a book on the grass. Can I see it?"

"Uh, yeah. Sure," I said while leading him out of the room, then out of the waterfall to my book on the ground.

While we were doing this, I was clueless about everything: the doors, the incidences, the waterfall, the boy, the moon, and everything else. While I was fetching the *Secrets of Aquarius*, there was only one thing I did know: I was really confused.

CHAPTER XIX

"Ah, here it is," the boy said, shuffling through the book. We had taken it back to his kitchen and were sitting at his table. "Right here," he continued, fingering the page. "It says that the Waterkeeper is only a descendant of the First One. Hmm...the dates are accurate. Waterkeepers went into hiding 3,915 years ago..."

That's what the place was! I thought.

"...hmmm mmm. Waterkeepers are only male. They start at age thirteen. If something should happen to him before his son takes over, the waterfall stops, and the world dies. And they do take care of the waterfall," he finished, still scanning the page.

"Wait. Are you saying all this stuff is accurate?" I asked.

"Uh, yeah. Shouldn't I know?" he replied.

"Well, I guess, but you never really introduced yourself. How should I know you should know?"

"My name is Deverex. I'm eighteen. The Clear Waterfall is what I look after, and this is my house, but you already knew that." He held out a hand and I shook it – reluctantly.

He kept scanning the pages of the book. Suddenly he looked up and said, "Who's this hic-cup guy?"

"What? No, it's not hic-cup, it's Hihc, right?" I replied.

He paused. "Who's this Hihc guy then?"

"Aren't you supposed to know? He's the guy who tried to trap the Waterkeeper 3,915 years ago," I said.

"That is *not* the name of the man who did that," Deverex refuted. "I guess I was wrong, this book isn't all accurate."

"Well then, what's his name?" I snapped.

"I can't just go *saying* it!" he said, sounding exasperated.

"Then write it down."

The Waterkeeper began searching cupboards, pockets, counters, and more for a piece of paper and a pen. When he finally found them, he wrote something down and gave it to me. It read:

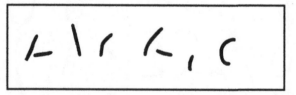

I had to squint to read his messy handwriting, but I thought I could make out a word.

"I'm sorry if you can't read it. I never have to write down anything, so my hand isn't really trained to write neatly. Can ya scrawl out a word?" he asked.

"No, I can read it. It's Hihc. See? H, then I, then a weird, messy H and C," I said.

"Ugh! No! That's not what it reads," Deverex exasperated.

"Then what does it say?" I huffed back.

Deverex sighed. "Fine, I'll say it, but only once. C'mere." He leaned in with the paper in his hand and motioned for me to lean in too. I did.

Deverex spoke in a harsh whisper and breathed, "The name of the family of that man…is Artic."

My hands started to shake. *Dr. Artic!* He is a descendant of the worst man that ever lived? Whoa! Had I been in danger my whole life?

The shock startled me so much that I fell over and tripped on the chair. The cloud-like floor seemed harder than usual. My breathing became uneven and my voiced cracked as I croaked, "Are you – are you sure it's – it's *that*?"

Deverex tightened his lips, closed his eyes and solemnly nodded. When he saw that I was struggling, he asked, "What's so surprising, Kyla?"

"That man lived!" I screeched.

Deverex held his breath for a few seconds. "What?" he whispered.

"*Yes!*" I grimly replied, staring at the floor through tears of fear. "I know his descendant. He's a top professor at Dinta! He despises me."

At this, Deverex's eyes widened with fear as he too became scared. He sat down in a chair and rested his head in his hands as I did. The room became silent as we both went into deep thoughts.

After a pause, he said, "You can't go back there Kyla. For your own sake."

I groaned. "But I have to! It's my home." I stood up. Deverex started toward me, and suddenly, I felt shorter.

"Do you know how *dangerous* this man could be Kyla? He could whisper death, he could be our world's downfall, he could…who knows? There are so many possibilities.

Good guys aren't the only ones who have powers Kyla – this isn't a fairytale. He could have as much power as me!" Deverex yelled, flustering about the room and waving his arms in the air.

I paused, thinking thoroughly about what the Water-keeper had just said. "So you're saying that Artic could have as much power as you?"

He shook his head. "Yeah, it's what I've been scared about this whole time. If I meet him, and I blow it, every-one's blown," he said, sitting down again and looking off to the side.

The shock hit me like a bus again. The world depended upon Deverex, and if he went, life as we know it would go too.

"Wow," I whispered, sitting on the cloud floor again with my hands in my lap. "So what do we do now?"

Deverex thought for a moment. "Tonight's the night of the full moon right?" he asked.

"Yeah."

"Then you have some work to do. I want you to go pack up everything you brought, and…and…go destroy your hammock or whatever you made. Then you need to wait until the moon rises. Meet me at the pool then. Go!" he said, then finished, "Now I have some work to do." He said the last part as he was walking out of the room. Since I was now very scared, I did not disobey.

It was hard trying not to be anxious as I waited at the poolside. It was dark now, but the moon hadn't quite risen. Thinking about it, I kind of wished that Deverex hadn't made this big plan to keep me safe when I went back to Dinta. I didn't want to go back. Not to Artic.

I put everything away now because the moon was rising. My eyes started searching for Deverex in the darkness, but to no avail. Suddenly, something grabbed my shoulder. I jumped and let out a little scream, which was embarrassing because it was only Deverex. He was in water form.

"Calm down, sissy, it's just me!" Deverex teased.

"Oh sorry," I whispered sheepishly. "So, what now?"

"You're gonna get baptized," he replied.

What did that mean?

"Whaddaya mean? Like by Luna or something?" I asked. "When?"

Deverex looked up at the rising moon. "Hmm. Not yet. I'll be back in a bit." And with that, his water body disappeared into the pool before I could protest.

I didn't like waiting much, but what could I do?

A little later, the moon was directly overhead and it made the water gleam mysteriously. I felt the hypnotism again. Oh no. My eyes crossed and suddenly I wasn't in control of myself. I - or, at least my person - started chasing the moon's reflection on the shore. But it kept moving, so I kept moving. Suddenly, I was at the waterfall.

I was very frightened by all of this - but I was not capable of doing anything. It was as if I had been drawn there. Against my will, with my face inches away from the pounding water, I stepped into the waterfall's thundering water.

The water was amazingly heavy, pounding on my body mercilessly. I felt as if my head and heart were being drowned by water and the pain was increasing. Finally, I collapsed. When I did, I was dragged under by the water.

And then I saw visions, or maybe I was dreaming? They were only a few seconds each, flashing images in my mind. First, I was on Grandmother's lap, and though the pictures were inaudible, I got the impression that she was telling me Luna stories. She held out a pocket watch, with an intricate carving of Luna on the face. That moon turned into the moon that I had seen beyond the waterfall, and then into the one in Deverex's chapel. Then I was flashed an image of a man I had never seen before, who had blonde-brown hair, beautiful blue eyes, round glasses, and a long nose. And just as quickly as he had appeared, he turned into Deverex. Then Deter flashed into my mind. His heart was pierced with the laser that had been stolen. And then, Dr. Artic, with his wild, white hair and flaring nostrils appeared in my mind. In my vision, out of complete and utter terror, I screamed.

Without warning, I snapped out of it, or maybe I awoke. Whatever happened, the visions were gone just as fast as they had come. Now I was floating in the pool, looking up at the big dome of sky, looking up at Luna. But this time, it wasn't a reflection.

CHAPTER XX

The next morning, I went to Deverex, who was staring at the falls. "I'm sorry I didn't wait for you for the whole safety-baptism thing. Stuff happened. It's a long story," I apologized.

"Whatcha mean?" he asked.

"Well you told me to wait, but I..."

"No, you were baptized. You went into the waterfall, remember?"

Oh.

"Was that really my baptism? Deverex, I saw..."

"Don't tell me!" he exclaimed. "Those are the secret sightings that Luna gives you at baptism. They're secret. For your eyes only."

Wow, I thought. "Like visions?" I questioned.

"Well – sort of, I guess. They're almost, kinda like hints to your destiny. So some of them are from the past."

"But Deverex, can you tell me what they mean? They were almost..." I started.

Deverex became flustered. "No. *Your* destiny. Yours. Only yours. It's a secret for you only – you. No one else should ever know what you saw. Now you should get going for Dinta. I have to go do stuff anyway."

And with that, he turned into his water form and disappeared into the water. I began heading for Dinta, thinking about the strange "visions" that could possibly tell me my destiny.

Once I got to my boat just outside of Dry Cove (I didn't see Deter), I started thinking about the visions in more depth.

The moon may have meant that I would well, I don't know, learn about my religion more or something like that. Maybe it was a sign that I should trust my religion more. In the end, I was pretty sure that it meant both of them.

I had no idea who the man was, or why he turned into Deverex, and even though I spent the most time thinking about that image, I remained clueless. The picture of Deter with his heart pierced by the missing laser was a very scary image. Could it mean that Deter would be killed by the laser's deadly powers soon? Even though I thought it meant that, I really hoped I was wrong.

Then the last image – Dr. Artic. I didn't even want to think about it, but I was afraid it meant something bad. Even if it meant I would be around him more often, that was scary, but it was even scarier knowing that it was probably something on a bigger scale – like if he would threaten my life or something really severe. After all, he was in the vision that meant my destiny.

The rest of the week passed very slowly. Nothing significant or spectacular happened at all besides being scared of Dr. Artic, which made for a very boring week.

I did not tell Awanata about the waterfall, and Deverex and everything else. Not because I was hiding it from her, but because I wanted to tell her when I knew more pieces of the puzzle.

Also, I started going to the waterfall every weekend, but Awanata wasn't too big on the idea of me sneaking out, or missing days that we usually hung out together.

I went late on Friday, so unfortunately I did not beat traffic. I got to the waterfall late at night. It was a new moon that night, so it was hard to see, but I managed to get beyond the waterfall to Deverex's house. He had set up a bed for me, since I was visiting so frequently, so I just climbed inside.

As soon as I fell asleep, it seemed it was morning again. I woke up to the smell of bacon and eggs. Deverex may have been isolated most of the time, but boy could he cook! I snuck a piece of bacon and then went into the fridge and cabinet and poured us both a glass of juice.

"Mornin' Kyla," Deverex said while tending to the simmering eggs.

I hummed a greeting back because I still had bacon in my mouth.

"Why weren't you here last week and why late this week?" Deverex asked.

While I was gathering the dishes and silverware, I replied, "Well, this week because of traffic, and last week Dr. Artic supposedly caught me up after curfew, so ya know, I had to stay 'cause of discipline rules."

"But were you up after curfew?" Deverex questioned.

He flipped the eggs and the sizzling sound filled the kitchen. I attempted to sneak another piece of bacon, but he swatted my hand away.

"No, I wasn't. It was actually four minutes 'till, and I

was just getting my books." I rolled my eyes at the pathetic thought of Dr. Artic.

Deverex nodded. "What did ya have to do? Stop stealing the bacon!"

"Had to tutor some stupid fourteen-year-old kid. But the thing is, I don't know who won the Ice War of 1412!"

Deverex let out a breathy laugh. By now he was serving the eggs and I was turning on the news in the other room. Deverex always had to have the news on, so that he knew if there was a flood somewhere, or a drought or conflict to be aware of.

We spent breakfast talking about things like the local sports teams.

Well, even though it was a weekend, Deverex wasn't off the job, so after breakfast he went through the waterfall to go do "Waterkeeper stuff." Meanwhile, I did little things like replenishing the bird feeder, which Deverex always found helpful. As always when alone on those days, my mind began to think.

Deverex had shown me that the doors I had discovered a few months back were his way of getting around. His big job as Waterkeeper was to make sure that the water supply was balanced everywhere in the world – which was an enormous job. The doors made it easier to get from place to place. Where did all the water come from? Why did the water supply never run out? The answer was the waterfall.

The book *Secrets of Aquarius* was pretty accurate besides the name Hihc.

I found out that Luna's vast importance was tied to the way she controlled water with the tides, using her magnetic field. But even though I knew all of this new information, giving me a glimpse of my world's secrets, I found myself more interested in something else – Deverex.

He was extremely kind and selfless, and occasionally humorous, but also stubborn at times. He was nice and understanding and so much more. Many of the virtues that he had were virtues I had always admired but not developed. There was something so secretive about him, but that had been his lifestyle for so long. I felt as though I was the only person he had ever opened up to before, so he almost didn't even know how to open up. It was almost as if he was always yearning, longing, for something more. And I was pretty sure it was a life outside of duty he longed for. But of course, that couldn't happen. He was destined to be a Waterkeeper, and it was already written in the stones and scriptures what his life would be. He had no say in his own fate.

The very first story Deverex ever told me was the one when he first left his home. He couldn't finish it because he had gotten too choked up. He had left a family behind. That was now clear to me, the sacrifice he made. He said that sometimes he would just close his eyes and wonder where his mother was.

Deverex was pretty much trapped. For him, there was no way out.

I felt bad for him. Yet still he was a great person. In

fact, he had become one of my best friends. There was something so different with him.

I was still thinking about this when he returned. "Deverex!" I cried, and then I rushed to him. Still feeling bad for him, I threw my arms around his neck and gave him a long hug.

Deverex was taken by surprise and didn't hug me back because of it. When I let go, I saw a very confused look on his face.

"Are you okay?" he asked worriedly.

"Yeah, are you? You were gone for an extra long time," I replied.

A look of pain and worry came over his face, and he sat down in a chair. "Kyla" he said with his face in his hands. "The laser! I've been thinking about it, and I think it's an even bigger deal than I realized. Somebody has it, and somebody evil." He stared off into the distance, facing away from my direction. I listened intently from a nearby chair. "The only way to be sure that no danger comes from it is to have it in our own possession," he continued, "but that's the most dangerous way there is, to get it from someone like that in person, exposing myself."

"Can you speak to Luna?" I suggested.

"Not directly. Not a full moon tonight."

"Well, maybe I can help you do this. I'm not water like you are."

Deverex thought hard for a full minute. Then, he looked up and said, "You know, that's not a bad idea. You wouldn't be as vulnerable as me, and should something happen to you the world doesn't end. What do you know about the laser?"

He squared up to me, and we were directly facing each other now. Our faces were inches apart, and I could see all of the seriousness and emotion in his eyes. I sighed, and started, "It was in a newspaper article..." I then proceeded to tell him all the details about the laser crisis that the article had given me. When I was done he asked me if there had been any other crimes that I knew of that could be linked to the laser situation. The only crime I could think of that had been local in Dinta was the bank robbery Artic had told me about.

"Hmm. I wonder if the guy was gonna use the money to pay people to help him or to make more lasers..."

"Sounds possible," I offered.

He was quiet for a second, and then shook it off. "I guess that doesn't matter right now. But it might help us later. Anyway, back on topic..." Deverex stared intently at me, and I shifted uncomfortably.

"What?"

"Kyla, I need your help to get the laser. I'll do some investigation on where it could be and you have to return each weekend from now on. But you must keep this a secret. And not just that you're gonna save the world from the laser, but about everything you know about me and the falls. Not one soul can know. You can't even think about it near others – not your mother, not your friends, not anyone. If you go around telling stories, people will think you're nuts. The government might get involved and you could get into some serious trouble. But what's even worse, is that there's gonna be someone who will think you're telling the truth and they could seek me out, and..." he sighed. "Do you understand?" he explained.

"I do."

"Do you swear to keep it a secret?"

"I swear, Deverex."

"Good. There's only about one thing that you don't already know."

A chill ran down my spine.

CHAPTER XXI

Deverex walked me to the top of the waterfall, and I saw the tall, wild grass blowing in the wind. For a minute we were silent. Deverex started to say something, but then stopped. He seemed to be on edge, almost waiting for something to happen, but I didn't know what.

"What Deverex? Tell me," I said.

"Well, you swore you'd keep me a secret right?" he asked.

"Yes!" I reminded, getting a little impatient.

"Um, well," he said and sighed.

"What!?"

"Okay, I didn't tell you this before because I thought I couldn't trust you. I didn't know who you were— well, not really. I wasn't sure, okay? But now I know you, and I can feel it, so..." he sighed. "C'mere."

I was very scared by this time. "What?" I asked, but I did what he said. He told me to stand on the edge of the land, right where the water on the falls began, and I saw how far down it was. "Whoa!" I shouted.

"Are ya ready?" he asked.

"For what?" I responded. But it was too late. Deverex pushed me down the waterfall. My scream pierced the air like a knife. What was going on?! Why had Deverex done that? But there was no time to think.

It felt as if gravity wasn't working, even though I was

falling. I felt like I was on a huge roller coaster, twisting and turning toward the ground. I felt weightless and I could feel my heart pounding in my chest. The energy was sucked out of me.

So I just kept falling and falling, not knowing when it would end, and felt sick to my stomach. I hardly had enough energy to scream. Falling down the waterfall that was many times taller than Dinta's boarding school, back to the ground, looking up and watching Deverex peek over the edge of the falls and then disappear. Without warning, the water met me, and all became dark.

The average person wouldn't have lived.

CHAPTER XXII

I woke up in my bed in Deverex's spare room, snug under the covers. Looking out the window, I saw it was the next morning. Sunday morning.

I got up, but suddenly winced in pain. It seemed as though a bad headache had developed. I changed and walked out to the main room, rubbing my head.

Deverex was standing in front of the TV, staring very seriously at the screen, taking in something the news was buzzing about. He must have heard me groan because he turned around and brightened up.

"Hey Kyla. Feelin' better?" he said.

"Um," I groaned. "Not really."

Deverex became a bit somber. "Sorry 'bout that. I was expecting a bit of this, but I thought you'd be a bit more durable."

Inside I was screaming, *What!? More durable?! Buddy, I fell off a cliff! Why'd you push me off the waterfall?! What were ya thinkin'!?* But outside I was calmer and just said, "What?"

"I knew you'd be a little bit not-your-best, but I didn't think it would be this much."

I paused, staring at him. "Okay, I'm confused, and I don't understand what you just said. So, I'm gonna ignore that," I said, talking slowly. My words slurred together slightly. "But why'd you throw me off the falls?"

Deverex started to say something, then stopped. He sighed, then said, "I'll tell you when you're feeling better. But until then, let's get some ice on your head because I need to go. It's urgent."

I nodded since I would probably understand better when my head wasn't throbbing. "That sounds good. But what's urgent, Deverex?"

"Some place called Dry Cove's got a huge forest fire. The place is so parched that they don't even have enough water to stop it themselves."

My natural instinct would have been to say, "Aw, well that's too bad." But something was somewhat familiar about Dry Cove. I was thinking so hard, but couldn't find a solution, and it only made my head worse. Finally, I gave in to all the confusion and pain I was feeling and began to cry (which, yes, did make my head feel worse). I cupped my head in my hands.

"Huh, Kyla, I'm so sorry 'bout all this," he said. I didn't respond.

"Dry Cove?" I whispered.

"Yeah...why?"

I closed my eyes and gritted my teeth. The confusion, the pain was overwhelming.

Deverex sighed. "Do you think you have a concussion Kyla?"

"I don't think so. It's more like a bad migraine. I've had a concussion before, I'd know."

Deverex nodded.

I had gotten my concussion when I first went to Dinta.

That's what happens when you walk into an Elements room on ice setting unprepared.

I was still lightly crying. "I'm so confused, Deverex."

Deverex nodded again. "I know how you feel," he sighed and then looked at the TV screen and sighed a bigger sigh.

"Look, I'm sorry, Ky, but I need to go. Let's get you situated and then I need to leave for Dry Cove," he finished.

I nodded. He helped me get situated on the couch. By the time he left, the room lights were off and I had a washcloth on my face with ice on my head.

Every once in a while, I'd look at the TV. The orange flames blazed, dominating the screen. They didn't go away for most of the time, but by the end, the fire was out. All that lay in the ruins of the forest was a pile of sticks and clay.

CHAPTER XXIII

The boy was scared. Confused. Frightened. Afraid for the life he once had, but now was destroyed.

"What have you done?" the boy said while scanning the destruction, his face turning into hard anger.

The old man stood, scanning the destruction with his scowling eyes and wild hair. But all he saw were dead trees and the mound of earth. There was no tidal wave, or water structure, or anything he wanted to see. "We didn't find him!" he boomed. "He never came!"

The boy was near tears now. Everything was destroyed. "But why, Grandfather?"

The old man gripped the laser tighter in his hands. "The fire would've attracted the Waterkeeper. I could've caught him when he came," he told the boy.

The boy dropped to his knees on the smoldering ground beside the man. He was crying now, as he collected some of the smoking earth into his palms. "But..."

"You fool!" the crazy old man roared. The boy hung his head low. "You were the one that told me there was clay here. I wouldn't have done this if it weren't for that. That meant the Waterkeeper was here." The man raged, "Of all the generations, you had to be the one who didn't want revenge! Revenge for being so close to the glory. Your father was better than you, boy. All of them, my grandson. You're the first! In a thousand generations! And you shall be the last!"

The man flustered about now, and the boy still hung his head low. Finally, the man reached a conclusion. He said, "I'm the only blood you have left, boy. You have nowhere else to refuge. Not this time. You will become my slave. Come now. Get to the boat. We have work to do and places to be."

The boy dropped himself to the ground, tasting the burnt earth. However, the crazy old man had no tolerance for his grandson's weakness; he thrust the boy onto his feet by his arms and walked away to the boat.

Still crying, the boy stayed where he was. He unveiled the distorted, ashy clay statue of himself that had been in his hand. He held it close to him. Because now, it was all he had left.

CHAPTER XXIV

When he came back, Deverex was very silent and deep in thought. He stayed that way the whole day. He was... grim. Disturbed. Uneasy.

My head began to feel better as the week progressed in Dinta. The ice had really helped.

Awanata didn't like how I was acting differently. I was being secretive, she said. I was just as aware of it as she was. But I didn't tell her anything. I needed to tell her when I understood it. How was she to understand if I didn't?

The next weekend I went back, my head mostly healed. When I got there Deverex was outside, studying the waterfall. I noticed that it wasn't pounding quite as hard, and it wasn't pouring as much water as usual. But even so, it was a big falls.

"Hey Deverex," I said while going to the entrance of the house, giving him a playful punch on the shoulder.

His eyes didn't leave the waterfall. "You feelin' better?"

"Yep."

"Good. Go unpack and then come back out. It's a follow-up to last week. Get dark clothes, hoodies and stuff," he said, then turned to me. "Things that'll cover up your identity," he finished.

I was taken by surprise and scared, yet at the same time, a rush of adrenaline went through me that made me smile. I hurried and obeyed Deverex quickly, because he had been awfully serious.

I put on black leggings and gloves, and a grey hoodie that could somewhat cover my face.

"Good," he said when I came out.

"Now, what are we doing, Deverex?" I asked nervously.

"I figured it out," he said with a grin.

"Figured what out?"

"The laser!"

My eyelids blinked and my jaw dropped. Now I was alert and listening.

"Dr. Artic has it!"

"What!?" I was astonished.

"I mean, think about it," Deverex continued. "That fire in Dry Cove was so big. That kind of fire doesn't start on its own. It must've started with a laser."

"Why Dr. Artic?" I asked.

"Well, he's sort of really evil, first of all, and I did some research. He wasn't at your school during that weekend. He took a 'vacation,' " Deverex said.

"To Dry Cove!" I finished.

Deverex nodded excitedly.

I continued, "So all we have to do…"

"All you have to do. *You.* Not me, remember?"

"Right. Sorry."

"Kyla, all you have to do," he said optimistically, "is sneak into his room and take the laser."

I rubbed my neck uneasily. "I dunno, Deverex. If I get caught, I don't know what they'd do. More than tutoring, that's for sure."

"But if you don't do it..." Deverex didn't finish. He knew I could finish the thought in my head. He sighed. "He's already done enough damage, Kyla. We can't let him do any more," he said.

I sighed. I knew he was right. I thought for a good minute, and then said, "What's the plan?" while straightening up.

Deverex grinned. "Good. And we start..." he said, taking my wrist, "...somewhere new."

He led me through his tunnels. There were turns and bends, but instead of a day's journey, we arrived on Dinta's campus in thirty minutes flat, and we were right in front of the professor's building.

"Do you know where his office is?" Deverex questioned.

"Yes," I replied.

"Do you know the plan?"

"Yes."

"All right. I'll meet you back here in an hour. If you need it, I have an escape door at the western corner of the building. Got it?"

"Got it."

"See you then." And with that, Deverex turned into water and fled down the downhill tunnel.

I looked out to the campus. It was dark and rainy. I pulled my hoodie mostly over my face and then ran through the clearing to the building. Straightening my back against it, I looked around. There was no one. I inched along until I came to the door. The building had

long been closed and shut down by now.

I tried the door. "Blast it! Locked!" I whispered to myself. I'd just have to hack the passcode.

Fingers on the pad, I tried to think of what Dr. Artic would make the password to the building. It would be a five-number combination.

Suddenly, the moon came out, peeking through the clouds ever so slightly.

For some reason, I subconsciously typed in "9-2-8-3-7" then "Enter."

"You have 30 seconds to enter the building," a robotic voice said from the keypad.

"Wow, it worked!" I whispered to myself. I rushed inside.

There was only about a square yard of space before there were staircases going up and down. That meant this wasn't the main door. It was the teachers' door.

I waited for my eyes to adjust to the lighting. I used the blue light from my watch to help me see.

It was 10:14. I had forty-six minutes to do this. It was all or nothing.

I raced up the stairs two at a time, my necklace bounding all around. At every turn, there was a landing before the stairs continued their ascent. After every two sets of stairs, a door entered onto a different level.

Racing, I passed floors two, three, and four, all the while whispering to myself, "Nine, two, eight, three, seven." I didn't want to forget the number because I would more than likely need it again.

Finally, my watch illuminated level five.

Level five was the level Dr. Artic's office was on. He was at the end of the hall – the top professor always got the biggest and best room.

I crept down the red patterned carpet with my hood still covering my face. Everything was so eerie. Dark. Empty. Every room looked like it was frozen in time. Everything seemed like it was moving, like it would swallow up the first soul that would dare enter, which, I realized grimly, would be *me*.

Trying unsuccessfully to push the fear aside, I stepped into Dr. Artic's room. My nerves took over, my body tensed up, and my heart raced. I was afraid for – well, I didn't even know what, but something bad.

Nonetheless, I knew what I had to do.

I started searching through drawers, boxes, shelves, and any nook that could fit the laser. But it was nowhere to be found. Time was slipping away and beads of sweat started accumulating on my forehead and upper lip. I flinched at every small sound I heard. I would have to get creative to find this thing.

I began to eye the big, centered tapestry on the wall behind the desk. It was grand. In the middle of the red background—matching with the room—was the big, yellow, "D" for Dinta. Sure enough, behind that D was a safe.

Figuring it couldn't possibly be this simple, I entered the same code as before: 9-2-8-3-7, and the safe opened. I got chills when I saw what was inside: The LASER!

Deverex had been right! The laser was right here!

Hurrying now, I took the laser and clasped it to the chain around my neck. After closing the safe, I rushed out of the room and shut the door.

Breathing heavily now, I rested my back against the door. It was still raining outside.

I checked my watch. It read 10:57. A chill ran down my spine. I would have to hurry to meet up with Deverex at 11:00! He hadn't wanted me to be late, otherwise he ran the risk of exposing his tunnel on the ground.

I raced down the hall and down the stairs, skipping most steps. The laser jangled on my neck. I didn't use the watch, because now my eyes were well adjusted to the light. Finally, I reached the bottom of the staircase.

Reaching the door, I once again entered 9-2-8-3-7 to exit.

"You have 30 seconds to exit the building."

I didn't even hear the robot voice finish. I tore out of that room fast as I could. It was starting to creep me out, and I had to hurry for Deverex.

I met him at the hole at 11:02.

"You're late," Deverex said as we started down the tunnel.

"Thank you for your unending patience and support," I replied sarcastically.

Deverex ignored that. "So did you get it?"

"Yes! It was in some vault."

"It is on your neck?"

"Yep."

"Good. Make sure to keep it away from me."

"I know. That's about your tenth reminder."

We went down the tunnel talking about this accomplishment and what we should do with the laser.

Near midnight, we arrived at the falls. Deverex had me put the laser in an offering box on the altar of Luna. He said it was to symbolize that we were doing this for Luna, for her people, and that we were always loyal. But we were going to keep the laser for now, rather than get rid of it somehow.

After that, I simply went to bed after being exhausted from an action-packed day.

CHAPTER XXV

I woke up late on Saturday morning, so Deverex and I had brunch together, discussing nothing but the laser. Once again, the news was buzzing about Dry Cove, but this time, the aftermath.

I finally figured out why "Dry Cove" sounded so familiar – Deter! I was very worried about him, but I kept it to myself because right then, Deverex and I had other priorities.

After brunch, Deverex and I tested the laser, in case it was a phony copy. We did not have to test it much to find that it was real.

Afterward, we had to decide what would be next, so we returned to the book of Luna and *The Secrets of Aquarius*. Deverex was searching for something in both books at once.

"So what now?" I asked.

Deverex sighed. "Well, we've got to keep an eye on Dr. Artic. Luna will be able to help me tonight."

"Wait, how do we keep an eye on Dr. Artic?" I asked.

"Simple. *You.*"

Oh...

"Wait, are you saying *I'm* gonna have to spy on a teacher?" I said.

Deverex replied, "Well, is there any other way? You'll just make sure he's not up to something and maybe pull a few sneaks. By the sounds of it though, you're not going to be doing any more mischief than you're used to."

That was probably true.

"Well...all right. Just give me like, the afternoon and I might have something."

"Okay."

That afternoon I swam in the pool, thinking of my own thoughts. Just none of it made sense. This whole thing was so confusing. And I felt like I practically had the puzzle solved, but I was missing the most important piece. I mean, I knew every single secret there was to tell, everything there was to know, but it just felt – wrong. But I wasn't sure if I'd ever find out.

When the moon was high in the sky and the sun had long been set, Deverex met me by the falls, the moon glistening on the water. I had to avoid looking at it, or else the hypnotism would set in.

"Luna's settled it," he said, approaching me. "It's time for you to be told."

I was taken aback. "What?" I asked nervously.

"Come with me."

In silence, Deverex led me through the falls to the temple I had seen the first time I entered the waterfall, grabbing the water as if he was opening a curtain.

I gulped as we walked in, because the way he was acting – it was different. Alarming. There was a sense of electricity in the air.

Deverex bade me to sit down in front of the pool with the moon face. I obeyed, but with hesitation and skepticism. Deverex sat beside me, our feet dipping the water and our eyes scanning the moon statue.

I had become very close to Deverex, and had gotten to know him very well. Almost never did I feel awkward around him, but now, I felt extremely conscious about myself. I was nervous and scared because I had a feeling that I wasn't prepared for what was going to happen.

"Kyla," Deverex said, meeting my eyes more than usual, "look at the moon in the water's reflection. You can almost tell who she is by looking at her."

Doing what Deverex said, I got a chill down my spine. When looking at Queen Luna's eyes in the water, I felt as if I was connected to her.

I could feel Deverex's eyes rest on me to my right.

"Everyone has some importance in the world. Everyone has a destiny."

His words were sudden after our silent pause, but even more startling were the words he said. What did he mean by them?

He must have felt my body tense up because he splashed his feet in the water so that the reflection wasn't as vivid. But, he went on, and took a deep, slow breath as if he was preparing to speak for a while. I could sense a story coming on.

And as he began to tell the story, it reminded me all too much of those stormy nights when Grandmother had told me stories about the "Children of the Stars."

And so the story began...

"Queen Luna was sad because up above the Earth, in

the place she was sentenced to live, it was lonely. And at this time, the world was still on fire because of the ray she stole from the Sun.

Emptiness overwhelmed her spirit as every day, she looked upon her destruction. And grief loomed about her head, looking at her loss. The anxiety in her caused things that had never been before because the grief was so intense. And there in the sky, Luna cried.

But behold, because once her grief-stricken rage ceased, something was left over. And it was water; the purest of water from her tears.

Queen Luna did not think much of it, so she thrust it down on Earth. But it did something magical: it defeated the fire. And in great rejoice and song, Luna responded.

The first drop of her tears became The First One.

The Earth was finally healed. When it was filled with water, strange things began to happen. Life began. And seeing this world's beauty, Luna sent the Children of the Stars there.

It was here on this world people have remained ever since then.

Luna still sends water. It is the Clear Waterfall."

Deverex turned back to me now.

"Everyone has a purpose, Kyla. Queen Luna makes everyone special, just like a drop of water."

I didn't feel like I had a purpose. I had been searching for sixteen years by now, and I still didn't know. I had given up on it a long time ago, but part of me always still wondered.

Deverex resumed, "Everyone has a destiny. Ultimately, it is polishing the stars for everybody. But there's a lot between now and then. My destiny is more – definitive. I'm the Waterkeeper." Deverex laughed a dry laugh at the end, but it was a sad laugh.

"Do you know your destiny Kyla? Do you know who you are deep inside?"

Deverex leaned toward me now, looking me in the eyes. But I couldn't meet his.

Deep inside, in a small drawer in my mind that I never let even myself open, I knew who I was.

But I shrugged to him, my face turned away from his. That shrug was a lie and Deverex knew it.

"Kyla, who are you deep inside?"

I looked away from him, and revealed something I'd never even revealed to myself, much less anyone else.

"I am Kyla Marine, daughter of Thetis Marine…"

It was getting hard to breathe. I didn't know if I would be able to continue.

I have always kept my past hidden from everybody, because it is ugly. I try to keep it hidden from myself, pretend it never happened. But I don't succeed.

"I pretend I'm this big, brave, daring person. But really I'm not. I pretend I'm so strong and fearless, but I'm not. It's because I'm scared that I act this way. It's because I'm scared that I do stupid things to seem brave and daring. It's because I'm weak that I act strong and because I'm…"

"Because you're afraid to be anybody else," Deverex finished for me.

He had read my mind.

"It's all I've ever known."

My eyes stung with tears. Deverex listened to me closely, eating up my every word. He was starting at me so intently that I thought his gaze would drill through my head.

But I didn't move my eyes because I couldn't make myself look into his. It was too painful. I just wanted to cry myself away from Luna. This religion stuff was heavy, too heavy at times, for me.

The story of my past began when I was two when my father and brother left. My life collapsed. Mother changed and I changed, and the hardness of life was revealed to me. I had already told Deter about all of this.

"But you're not just a failure, Kyla. You have a destiny and you're something more. Look again inside yourself. Who are you?" Deverex insisted. He leaned even closer now, making me feel claustrophobic.

I put my head in my hands and shook…"No!"

Deverex stood up and pulled me by the arm up out of the pool and locked gazes with me.

"Kyla" he said softer and slower.

"You are…a Waterkeeper!"

Suddenly, the room began to spin around me and my knees couldn't support my weight anymore. I collapsed onto the stone floor, my eyes watering and my breath becoming uneven.

I was a Waterkeeper?! What?! It didn't make sense, it couldn't be! I didn't have any water-controlling superpower or special mortality. I just knew I wasn't a Water-keeper! Then I'd have to be related to Deverex....

But I *knew* I wasn't a Waterkeeper. Deverex allowed me a moment to let it sink in. But then, he offered his explanation.

"Kyla, you're not – well, you're not a full-fledged Wa-terkeeper. You're like, half-Waterkeeper because you were born second. I, the first born, am the only guardian of the falls. You're...not."

He continued, "Your body is made of special water, like me, though. You still have magic, it's just deeper within you. You're special because usually there's only one child, but you're the second."

"This is what I was trying to show you when I threw you off the falls. A normal person would've been killed completely, but you just got a headache. And when I saved you in the waterway, it was because I could see the special water in you that told me you were my sister. You survived the hole to get here because of the magic water within you too."

"I'm sorry that this is so much to take in at one time, Kyla, but Luna said that you had to find out tonight. I'm the brother that ran away with your father when you were two. Your father and your brother – and you – are Waterkeepers. I'm your brother, Kyla."

I couldn't believe it. I just sat there trying to breathe, shaking as if I were dressed for summer in the middle of winter. But I was shaking with fear and hurt. I was hurting because I had based sixteen years of my life on false information—sixteen years of life wasted.

"Why couldn't you have told me?" I said, my voice wavering and cracking.

"Because even though you're my sister, I couldn't tell you right away. There are only a few people in the world that can keep this kind of secret, the secret of the falls and of our family, probably only you and me."

I had to make myself remember to breathe. "What about Father?" I croaked.

Deverex just stood there, stunned and silent.

In my wishes and dreams, I had called my father lots of things: Big Daddy-Oh, Daddy, Big Joe. In my daydreams we had been close, we had played ball and gone to the park together, him watching my Elements games and cheering at my life. That's what I had missed the most, what I longed for from my core. I desperately needed that extra love that my mother had never given to me. But that relationship with him had never developed.

And now, I wanted to know.

Deverex seemed uncomfortable. He started to rub the back of his neck nervously. Finally he sighed. "This may be a lot, but come with me."

I started to get up, but my knees were so weak from shock that they couldn't support me and I fell.

Deverex helped me up and then led me outside, back to the pool by the falls. I was confused. I didn't see a man magically appear, or swim up from the water. There was nothing. It was the same as it had been five minutes ago.

My eyebrows scrunched together. Staying silent, I

looked at Deverex. He knew what I was thinking: What?

Deverex's demeanor became solemn. He looked at me then cast his eyes downward, then at me again, and down again. At last, his eyes locked with mine, and he took his hand out of his pocket and gestured to the water.

I looked at the water, and my heart broke. I didn't know what else the world could do to me, and since the blow was so new, I just nodded my head, staying calm and neutral on the outside. But on the inside, I felt an awful pit in my stomach and poison was being fed into my heart.

I understood now.

Deverex carried me back to the house and set me down on the couch. I was too weak to do it myself. He sat in a chair beside me. I could tell he wanted to know what I was thinking but I was off in a trance.

My father was dead.

I couldn't believe it. He was dead. He wasn't lost, because he couldn't be found; he was gone. I didn't know what to think. The thing that I had needed and dreamed of my whole life was gone. *Never* to be found...

Deverex had revealed this by gesturing to the water, and it made sense. My father had been a Waterkeeper too – that's why he had left. He had taken Deverex with him to be the next Waterkeeper. But his body was now eternally water, in the bottom of the pool of the Clear Waterfall.

No sweet nicknames, no big hugs, no Elements cheers. It couldn't even be a fantasy anymore. All of my daydreams were at the bottom of the pool.

"Deverex," I croaked, snapping out of it, "when did he die?"

"Five years ago when I was thirteen. I began my duties, and he died, just as it was written."

I nodded. It was silent for a minute.

Everything was explained now. I knew all of it. This was exactly what I had wanted, but now I wished I hadn't wanted to know, because it hurt too much.

"Ya know, how 'bout you just go to bed? It's been a big day."

That was for sure.

I nodded and let Deverex help me to my room. Then I climbed in bed.

I spent the night staring at the ceiling trying to find comfort that was gone, not just lost. My father was dead—unbelievable. I had tried to pretend that he was just working for the government in a secret location, still alive, quietly loving me from far away. But I couldn't make myself believe it. I didn't think he had loved me. He never had done anything except keep me longing for nothing. That was what killed me—the imaginary thing that I had loved all my life that didn't love me.

I didn't cry or sleep that night. I felt numb. *At least I have Deverex.*

CHAPTER XXVI

I woke up late the next morning. It still hadn't sunken in completely. But I was fine with that; I didn't want it to.

Deverex let me be prickly and out of it. That really helped.

But it was so weird – Deverex was my brother? I had already developed somewhat of a love for him – a friendly love, *not* a romantic love – but to think of him as a brother was – weird. I liked it. I was glad he was my brother. Now I had someone to try to fill the fatherless gap in my heart. I liked the fact that I had a brother, and I really liked that Deverex was that brother. At least I found one half of my missing family. But for some reason, I thought it would take a long time to develop a sisterly love toward him, and him a brotherly love toward me. I didn't know why.

Being hazy like I was that day, I sat at the table in a trance, thinking about this, while Deverex got lunch ready. He started to get plates out of cupboards and forks out of drawers.

"Deverex?" I said suddenly.

"Yep?" he said, not looking at me and continuing to get plates out.

"What was Dad like?"

Deverex turned to me, halfway through opening the utensil drawer.

"Are you ready to talk about it?" he asked, making

more eye contact with me than usual.

I nodded, even though I wasn't really sure.

He walked over and sat down in the chair next to me – not across from me – and let out a big sigh. He crossed his arms and slouched in the chair.

"What was Dad like…" he whispered, locking his head to the side as if in a daze.

"Well," he said, returning his gaze to me, "he was very generous, and selfless – oh, very selfless – and caring and strong – especially strong."

"Did he train you to be a Waterkeeper?"

"Yep," Deverex replied, nodding. "Yep. I started when I was nine. He showed me the tunnels and taught me the way of the water."

"He really cared about me. He loved me so much. He really wanted his son to fulfill the task of our family successfully and happily. He just wanted his son to love the life he was bound to live." Deverex said slowly, deep in thought. Sometimes while talking he would pause or look at the wall in a trance, as if reliving the words he spoke.

"And do you?" I asked softly.

Deverex was obviously taken by surprise. His eyes got wide and locked with mine, and then he looked down. His eyebrows scrunched together as he was thinking and he sighed and bit his lip. More thinking. Uneasily, he readjusted his crossed hands so that they were under his arms and only his thumbs were visible. He leaned back and forth and back and forth in his chair, thinking hard.

I was sad that it was taking him this long. Did he not love his life?

Finally, he looked up - but not quite at me, a little to the side.

"I would say that—well—" Deverex stopped, and sighed again. "I mean, sometimes I wish I could have a normal life and ya know, but..." he let out another sigh. "I do love the life I live."

Thankfully. Finally! But it was unnerving to see that he was so hesitant. And was he really being honest?

There was a silent pause.

"Deverex, why are you letting me be so...prickly today?" I asked, ending the silent pause.

Deverex's arms resumed their crossed position as he said, "Because you just found out. And this is what my dad did to me when I first found out." He looked to the other side, again in a daze.

"He sorta just let me have at him, and it really helped. So now this is what I'm doin' to you."

"What'd you find out?"

"Well!" Deverex grunted. He threw his head back as though exasperated and then started playing with his fingers, chin on his chest.

"It's...sort of upsetting when...you learn that...your whole life is planned for you and there's nothing you can do about it."

Deverex looked away from me, blinking frequently, as if annoyed. But I was pretty sure he was blinking back tears.

"Well, thank you for being patient with me," I said softly.

Deverex turned back to me, letting go of his anger and hurt.

"Yeah."

There was another long pause, this one very long. Deverex leaned forward, looking at me. I could tell he was waiting for another question. But I didn't have anything else to say. Deverex started thumping his heels and shaking his knees. He leaned back and forward in his chair looking in the other direction than me, pulling his mouth to one side, then checked his watch. He did this about twice. I didn't move. Abruptly he stood up and started out the hallway.

"Deverex?" I said.

Deverex stopped right before the doorway and sighed. With a neutral face, he partially turned around and calmly said, "Yes Kyla?"

I started to say something but stopped, and then did that again. I wanted to tell him something from my heart, from my soul, but I was afraid to.

Finally, I whispered, "I love you."

Deverex's face softened in the best of ways and became very serene and calm. He smiled for the first time that day—a real, genuine warm smile.

"I love you too."

And with that, he left to go do the duties of a Waterkeeper, the great and powerful ruler of the tides, leaving me alone in the dimly lit room.

CHAPTER XXVII

I left for Dinta before Deverex got back that night, and snuck into my dorm as foxlike as I could. Monday came, and it was hard to concentrate. I had some other big thoughts on my mind of course. And while I was day-dreaming in classes, I made up my mind: it was time to talk to Awanata.

At lunch, I sat across from her in our regular booth. At first she ignored me, continuing to text on her phone.

"Hey Awanata."

No response.

"Blue."

She glanced up, then quickly back down.

I sighed. "Look Awanata, I know you're mad. And you have a right to be. I've been a jerk, and I...I know it. But I can explain everything, okay?"

She set her phone down with a thud. "*Really?*" she questioned, looking mad and doubtful.

"Yeah," I said, "down to every detail. It might sound a little far-fetched at first, but you've gotta trust me."

Awanata picked up her light blue phone again.

I sighed again. "Look, you're still my best friend, and I still want to be yours. Don't give up on me Awanata. If you want an explanation, come by my dorm after last class. Katrina will still be away at her sister's and Myrtle will be at her book club."

Awanata looked up from her phone.

"It better be a good explanation!"

And with that, she picked up her lunch tray and left.

"So what's been up lately?" Awanata asked as she threw a ball up in the air and back, her head hanging off my bed.

"So much," I breathed, tipping two of the four legs of my stool up off the ground. "I mean, I'll start from the beginning, but first you have to believe me. It'll sound crazy like I've gone mental or something, but please trust me, Awanata, okay?"

"Okay."

"Swear?"

"I swear Kyla, just tell me!"

I began to get nervous and feared she wouldn't believe me, but...

"I'm a Waterkeeper."

Awanata stopped throwing the ball. Then, she twisted so she was facing me and sat upright.

"What?" she asked with a very serious expression on her face.

I told her the whole story from beginning to end, including my fall from the waterfall and Deverex and Dr. Artic – even sharing my religion with her. It took a long time. By the end, the sky behind Awanata was growing dark.

Awanata was like a sister to me and always had been. She had always believed me and I had always believed her.

Now, for the first time ever, her trust in me was shaken.

"I mean, it *does* sound pretty far-fetched. Sounds like you've gone way off the edge," she admitted. I just stared at her with pleading eyes. "Well, I mean I *want* to believe you Kyla, that'd be awesome, but...what proof do you have?"

That was a question I couldn't really answer...except...

"I'll take you to the waterfall."

I needed her help, but first I needed her to believe me. On Friday after school, Awanata and I took a boat down to Dry Cove. We had made up, so we spent most of the time laughing and talking...until we got to the hole.

I had seen the destruction of the wildfire before, but Awanata hadn't. The land was flat now, with dead trees everywhere. The town had been destroyed. We both became very grim, for the place had been abandoned. The fire had burned five-sevenths of the land.

I led Awanata to and through the hole. To keep her safe during the journey through it, I dampened her face and hair with water from a bottle I had filled in the pool. Before I went in, I took a look around. The place brought tears to my eyes. Deter had surely died in the fire. At least I had Awanata and now Deverex.

Wishing to escape the place of destruction, I plunged into the dark hole.

I met Awanata at the wall. She was paralyzed, looking up at the stone wall that seemed to reach to the heavens.

"Are you okay?" I asked her. "Did something go wrong in the hole?"

"No," she replied. "That's why I'm amazed."

I laughed and proceeded to push the exact rock to expose us to paradise.

Just one step into paradise and Awanata became paralyzed again.

"I'm dreaming," she whispered, "I'm dead, somehow." She couldn't move.

"Deverex!?" I yelled. He was nowhere to be seen. My eyes darted all over the place, but he was not in sight. "Deverex!?"

I turned around just in time to see Deverex, in water form, sneak up from behind a tree and hit Awanata in the back of the head!

Awanata made a painful sound, and then fell to the ground.

Deverex transformed into human form and approached me in a way that made me feel very small. His nostrils flared with anger. He was obviously extremely angry. His eyes' hold on mine was so strong I couldn't tear away and I felt like I would turn to stone.

I started backing up. "Deverex, what did you do? Will she be okay? Deverex!?"

"Get into the house...*now*." His voice was as strong as his stare.

Once we were inside, the storm unleashed.

"Kyla, how *could* you? *Who* is she, why'd you tell her?! We had a deal, I thought I could trust you!"

"Deverex, she's not what you think! You can trust her! She's different! We need her help and we can't do this alone!"

"Kyla, you can't trust people. People are selfish, unsympathetic things. No one, *no one* is capable of keeping this secret except you and me. Oh wait, *not* you because you went and told anyone you thought you could trust! In fact, I bet you told *everyone*! I bet that if I went and looked in a newspaper, it would be about you and your golden findings, wouldn't it?!"

"Deverex, that's not true! I only told her, we had to sooner or later! I can handle this, you can trust me!"

"*Prove it!*"

"Deverex, you're not as smart as you think you are. You're not as sharp as you think. You're not always right!"

"Oh...Really?"

"See? Yes! That's what I mean! You're not always right, Deverex. You think you know everything about everything. You think you know what the world is like but you don't! I've actually lived in it! You've just been in isolation the whole time with no one to tell you how to get a personality!"

"Well, I'm starting to think you don't give me enough credit. I supply the world with life!"

"Yet, you don't supply yourself with one! Everything that comes out of your mouth is, oh, this will happen, oh this is how it is, how it has been, how it always will be! Deverex, how would you know more about people than me? Hate to break it to ya buddy, but you're basing everything on 4,000 year-old information! Some people have *changed*!"

"People don't change, Kyla. They never have and they never will."

"See!? That's exactly what I mean! You're wrong on this one!"

"Well, at least I don't go making promises I can't keep!"

"You don't give the world another chance. You isolate yourself. I've lived in society my whole life; you've lived separate from the world for 3,915 years. You don't know anything about anybody!"

For the first time since our fight began, Deverex stopped.

"You're right. I don't know anything about anybody. Because I was dumb enough to trust you."

And with that, he walked away, the air from the room still hot from our fight. Fighting back my own tears, I returned with Awanata to Dinta. I didn't want to see Deverex's face again.

At home that weekend, I started replaying what went down in my head. I had been nasty, but he had been too. It bugged me that Deverex had just assumed that I was wrong. But the truth was, some people really had changed and Deverex wasn't giving some people the chance that they deserved. Perhaps I was wrong about Awanata helping us, but I knew her as well as I knew myself, and I knew the secret was safe with her.

But of course, it didn't matter because she didn't remember anything, thanks to her whack to the head (through the weekend she healed with an ice pack on her head).

I stayed mad throughout that weekend, but through the next week I decided that possibly, Deverex had been traumatized by his isolation and didn't know any better of humans. Maybe he had already gone out on a limb with me and he just wasn't ready to get to know Awanata.

Maybe we had both been wrong.

But maybe I was just wrong.

No, *he* was wrong too.

I didn't return to the waterfall for a month, because I couldn't make up my mind on the situation and I truly didn't know what to think. I kept trying to think about it, staying up late some nights staring out into nothing, but my heart and my mind - and something else I couldn't pinpoint - couldn't harmonize. The whole thing was like a bad itch on my brain - it kept bugging me but it wouldn't go away.

But I missed Deverex. At first, I tried not to admit it, but I did. Now that I had this whole Waterkeeper thing in my life, it was hard imagining my life without it. I missed just talking to Deverex, teasing him but also doing serious things with him. I just - missed him. He was my brother, a part of me. And I cared about him. But once again, my thoughts could not agree.

Back at the waterfall, Deverex was having a tough time. Chores seemed harder, longer, and it was as if there was a bad itch on his brain. He kept thinking about his fight with Kyla, and he missed her. She was his sister. He cared about her. But he had made up his mind: he could not trust her, or anyone else, and his water was thicker than the blood he shared with Kyla.

CHAPTER XXVIII

About a month after the night I fought with Deverex (I still hadn't gone back), it was the night of the full moon. But it was cloudy so the moon had no effect in the sky. I lay in my dorm on the couch, throwing a ball up and down. Very mesmerizing considering it was such a simple activity.

Then, the phone rang. But since it was late, even on a Friday night, this surprised me. And it wasn't a cell phone, it was the room phone.

I answered it hastily so it would not wake up my roommates on the other side of the wall (not because I wanted to do something nice for them, but because they would never let it go if it actually woke them up, annoying idiots that they are).

"Um, hello? Who is this?"

"Hello Kyla. This is Dr. Artic…"

You've got to be kidding me.

"…Now I know that you are aware that Awanata Blue had a concussion not too long ago and has been actively trying to recover."

"Yeah…"

"Well, unfortunately, she slipped down the stairs today and hit her head again. Her condition is not good. We just got her to the hospital wing, and you being her best friend, we thought it proper that you come down immediately. Could you please come down to the hospital wing as soon as possible?"

Oh no, Awanata! It made sense because we hadn't had a class together that day. So I wouldn't have known she was hurt until now.

"Yes, I'll be down as soon as possible! Thank you!" I said, making feeble efforts to hide my panic. Then, I hung up the phone, slipped on a sweatshirt and quickly left.

Before this whole giant Waterkeeper mystery sprang up, I was never afraid. Fear was foreign to me. Before, I was a daring, fearless, unimportant citizen. But things were different now. Now, I had encountered fear more, and I figured I must be more vulnerable to fear now that I had become so familiar with it.

I made my way cautiously but swiftly down the halls. All the doors to the other dorms were either silent or barely stirring, with the only voice from within the muffled mutter of a movie playing.

The elevator was easier to take, but it would take me more time to get to the hospital wing. So, I would have to use the back corner stairs to get to "the bridge," which was a single hallway that linked two buildings on campus. From outside, it looked like an indoor bridge. It's a pretty self-explanatory name. Then I'd take an elevator to the hospital wing.

But I hate the back stairs. They're dark, unclean, and just eerie. *It's for Awanata*, I remembered, and repeated that to myself the whole way down just to concentrate on something besides the dirty words on the walls and the utter darkness.

I usually like the bridge, with its glass walls to see outside. However, with the circumstance of being vulnerable to fear, the evil hollowness of night, even through glass – was chilling.

Then after that, I took an elevator down to the hospital wing. Even the elevator, awfully empty, was scary to me. At least the lights were on.

The hospital wing consisted of a main desk in the entrance (right outside the elevator) with three hallways branching off, forming the shape of a T.

I walked up to the front desk. As I began to say I was here for Awanata, I noticed something. The worker at the desk, probably a student or intern, looked quite familiar. Not an "oh, have I seen you at the gym lately?" type of familiar, but an unknown familiar. An eerie familiar, yet even more eeriness. I couldn't see much, thanks to the sports cap he was wearing, and he wouldn't look at me even though he knew I was there. But that bit of his face, his posture, his presence...

I must have been really paranoid, because everything was eerie to me. *Nothing is scary,* I told myself.

Instincts are hard to ignore. It's impossible to "hum" them away.

"Uh, Awanata Blue?" I stated.

The boy was hesitant, tense, and then he got up and began walking down the longest hall. I realized how quiet the hospital wing actually was.

Awanata's room was the last room in the wing. My guide stopped and gestured toward the door.

Okay, I thought. *This is really weird.* And he had gestured towards the door rather than opening it and leading me in to see Awanata.

Stupid paranoia! I turned the handle, and for a millisecond, I got a shock of intense fear. But it was only for a millisecond. And my hand proceeded to open the door.

I stepped in. It was pitch black, although I barely had enough time to process that fact before a strike of pain hit my head and my consciousness gave way to even more darkness.

All of a sudden, the room was dimly lit and made of stone – top to bottom. It was a small square room, which looked like it wasn't kept up. But these things were not important to me.

A laser was pointed at my head, just about an inch away.

Dr. Artic was holding the laser.

My whole body tensed up and within a split second, my heart was beating 100 miles a minute. An awful flood of despair came over me as I realized that nothing I could do would stop Dr. Artic and that I was about to lose my life. It was just a matter of when now. I realized that I had been a fraud – I had never known what to fear – until now. I had never truly known fear before. Not like this. Right now, I was afraid for my life. And only now, while experiencing the realization that my life might end right now, did I realize the value of life itself.

It's a scary feeling. It's not a feeling at all, actually. It's when your heart and soul fight for breath in the sea of death. And you are changed – forever.

I expected every second to me my last, when suddenly, Artic took a step back and mumbled:

"Kyla Marine. Do you know why you are here?"

Deter was in the room, but he wouldn't look at me.

I didn't reply.

"Obviously not," Artic whispered. Then, he said something I never saw coming.

"I know that you are a Waterkeeper and I know that you know that I am a descendant of the Second One."

"When you met Deter, you two discussed the Children of the Stars. Therefore, he told you that he believes in Luna's Way, and therefore you told him you believe as well. Did you know that the only people on Earth that believe in Luna's Way are the First and Second Ones?"

A dead, cold silence was ruled by fear. Or maybe it was the atmosphere in the room.

"Oh right," Artic laughed, "Deter is my grandson."

So much shock and fear filled me from within that I felt numb. I started shaking.

"What?" I whispered. "Deter?"

Deter looked at me for a second then turned away. I could see he was on the brink of tears.

"Oh, don't worry for the boy!" Artic hissed. "He's been through much already. His mother died when he was a child and his father recently. I'm...sure you read the newspaper article about him?"

Deter's father was the man who had made the laser!

"Yes, my son," Artic said regretfully, "died from breathing in poisonous chemicals while making the laser. And he stole from the bank to make it too. But I am proud of him! He died with honor carrying the family name. Where Deter, he is an embarrassment, a disappointment, a mistake – a disaster! And yet, it is possible he could be the most important Second One in 3,915 years!" At this, Dr. Artic made a cry of despair.

"But *you!*" he resumed, "You may be my last hope." He tightened his grip on the laser. "So...tell me...where is the Waterkeeper?!"

I was in such shock that I thought I would break down and die on the spot. So many emotions were tearing me apart from the inside that I thought I was going to collapse and fall apart. The beginnings of tears stung my eyes.

"*Tell me!*" Dr. Artic boomed, louder than ever before.

I couldn't tell Artic. I owed it to Deverex. I really was sorry for what I had done. And this would mean the end of the world. *No,* I thought. *I will* not *tell him, even if it means I will die. He is my brother.*

At my silence, Dr. Artic pushed the surface of the unlit laser to my forehead, pushing my head into the stones behind me. This hurt very badly, but it was the least of my concerns. There was that rending feeling again, with a laser to my head.

"Where is he?!" Artic hissed.

With all the guts and force and courage I could squeeze out of my weakening mind, I just closed my eyes. Silent. Only now I realized my hands were tightly cuffed near my back.

Dr. Artic's arm retreated from my forehead. To my relief, that sort of made me want to break down and cry. Muttering oaths and stomping his feet, flailing his arms, Artic raged at me and at his family's past and at Deter, and about everything else. I just remained still with my head against the dusty, rough stone wall.

Artic kept trying again and again to get the information out of me, threatening to kill my mother or Awanata or anything he could think of. I just stayed silent.

Once Artic seemed to be done with his fit, he went to the corner of the room and quietly fought with Deter. After a few words, Artic took a breath and slowly turned to me.

"I will give you fifteen seconds before I end this for good!" His words practically branded me.

At this, with only fifteen short seconds of life still in me, I opened my eyes and looked up to the ceiling and prayed to Queen Luna.

I prayed for my mother's soul, such a determined soul, that she would know I'd be okay and that this was my choice and that someday, maybe we could be reunited, polishing the stars, or somewhere special. I prayed that she'd be okay and I thanked Luna for her and everything she had ever done for me.

I prayed for Deverex, that he would succeed in keeping the waterfall and all the waters of the world stable and controlled and that he would pass it on to his son smoothly. I prayed that he would be okay and know that I'm okay. I asked Luna to make him happy one day, maybe not on Earth, but eternally happy in the rest of life. I expressed my thankfulness to Luna for letting me meet him before my soon-to-be untimely death, for he was my beloved brother. Most of all, I just prayed for his soul.

I prayed for Awanata. I had abandoned her. *Protect her, Luna.* Awanata was a better person than me, and didn't deserve this pain. She was going to be alone in a world of fear, and hatred, and death. Because of me. I prayed for her safety and happiness, and that maybe she would be all right, strong, spared from the pain of death like I was in the midst of now.

I prayed for Dr. Artic, maybe he could be forgiven one day or change his ways. Because honestly, I felt bad for him. He was just a sad old man whose family had been without love since the beginning of time. And without love, he just turned to madness and hatred. People without love do bad things.

I prayed for Deter, because even though he was from the same family as Artic, he was capable of loving. His love had just been extinguished (or at least attempted to be), locked up, and not allowed to rule like it should.

I prayed for *me.*

I prayed that this was the right decision, to die, that I could polish the stars with Grandmother one day (as well as with mother, Deverex, and Awanata), that I could be forgiven of my sins. I thanked Luna for the healthy life I had lived, for the school that I had gone to. For the food I had eaten and the water I had cleansed myself with, for the family that I had dearly loved. I prayed that one day

I would be peaceful and happy in eternal life, and that all of this would be worth it.

With about two seconds of life yet to live, I noticed that the ceiling was darker than the rest of the room. No, it was...wet. Increasingly so...

I continued to pray.

At one second left, my body relaxed, stopped shaking, prepared for the unwanted relief soon to rule my soul.

Then, with less than a second left, a waterfall fell from the ceiling. The water formed into Deverex!

CHAPTER XXIX

Once again, my heart was pounding and my blood froze! Deverex, in his water form, stood between me and the laser.

The air in the rooms was so tense that it was hard to breathe in, as if it were stuffy.

Everyone's eyes were frozen on Deverex, marveling at how majestic his body moved, how the water circulated in him, how there was an atmosphere about him that could make a sinner drop dead in awe.

I swear my gut dropped so low that it drilled through Aquarius's core the moment Dr. Artic's mouth broke into a wide grin.

It had been a trap. Artic knew that if I didn't tell him straight up where Deverex was, he could threaten me. And then, Deverex would come and save the day.

It would have been better if I had just died. Deverex wouldn't have any interruptions and the world would run more smoothly and we'd all just continue our pretty little lives in this big world, never knowing about the Truth. The Truth can be deadly.

It was deadly.

And that's where I went wrong. I disobeyed the Laws Written in Stone that people had blindly lived by for 3,915 years. I had always questioned the Truth. I tried opening a door that was never meant to be opened, tried to follow a path that was never meant to be traveled on. I even opened the door and found out the Truth, only to find it is dangerous. Not just to me, but to every living being on this planet.

Deverex had foolishly come to save me. But now, he was exposed. If Artic was to kill him like he wanted to, the waterfall would stop flowing, and it would only be a short matter of time before the world would shut down, wither, and die, just like a plant.

It was my fault. My fault for finding the waterfall, my fault for following Deverex into that waterway, my fault for finding that door to start it all. It was me who proved Artic's final piece of evidence, as a follower of Luna, because I couldn't keep my mouth shut. I had been so naïve, trusting everyone. While I still believed Awanata could have kept the Secret, Deverex was right. People don't change; they haven't yet, at least. Deter was my proof—I wasn't sure if he was innocent or not, but I liked to think so, yet alas, it had cost me just the same. It had cost Deverex and me, and thinking back, I knew that I had never been fair to Deverex. I had been stubborn, selfish, and stupid.

But here we were, with the air electrified and everyone stunned frozen in that damp, rocky cell, located in who-knows-what latitude of the globe.

Only now I realized how majestic Deverex truly was. In his water form, he seemed more god than human. His movements and light cast a spell of wonderful hypnotism, a beautiful mesmerization. The sight of him made you want to relax your eyes into a haze. His very existence was awesome, and just the terribly rending way he moved could make someone collapse within. His horribly beautiful movements showed bursting power, strength, and importance.

There, in that room, Artic had the power of the world in his hand. He had the laser. He had only to aim and...

I'm sorry Deverex. I'm so, so sorry, I thought as I squeezed my eyes shut. I couldn't bear to watch.

But Artic hadn't shot the beam. I waited for what seemed like an eternity, but no laser!

It became clear that Artic wasn't going to shoot the laser! But why not? Surely he knew it was powerful enough to kill Deverex. And he had gotten over the initial shock of seeing Deverex, clearly, shown by his slimy smile. Alas, Artic shouted, "Deter!"

Deverex knew something wasn't right now. He became hesitant. Despair punched the pit of my stomach.

Upon his request, Deter passed Artic another contraption now from the corner of the room. It was longer than my forearm, and thick. It looked blue. I found it ironic that a holy color would be used against a holy being.

"Noooooo!" I screamed.

Artic shot.

The hatred from Artic was so powerful that, when channeled into this gun, froze Deverex right in front of my eyes. He froze into a solid ice figure. And like a fated domino, he fell backwards towards me, and cracked nearly in half.

Words can't explain emotions as powerful as mine right then. I shook dramatically, and let out one cry. One cry of pure anguish, regret, loss, and pain. I dared to stare at him. His body had a crack from when it fell, from the left hip to the right shoulder. Not broken, but cracked. What's the difference though, honestly? He was dead.

Dead.

The world's source of life had fallen down dead at my feet.

Artic proceeded to drag him out of the room, down some hall I couldn't see, while Deter took me up another hall. We didn't speak. My eyes filled with shocked tears. Deter put my chain around some other ground-level hook. It was a small room in what I finally recognized to be Dry Cove. I had a small slit window right next to me. Just a torture method, to show me an unreachable escape. And desolation.

Wait – that was the thing. Since the tragedy, many volunteer workers had planted all these trees and everything to help Dry Cove. The news had said that Dry Cove finally felt okay. I saw some trees now. They weren't green, they were brown. Withering...*dying*.

They were dying! Since Deverex had died, the waterfall had stopped, and the world was on a path to becoming a graveyard, and it was already starting to happen!

Because of me!

I actually considered killing myself for a minute. It was the only way to escape – but no – I didn't deserve to escape. I deserved to watch the world die around me.

I looked at the only thing that dared to shed light—the moon. It was full tonight. So Luna had a front-row seat to her servant's end. All I did for a while was just look at her. It's stupid that I did. I should've feared her wrath, but I didn't. I just looked at her and thought.

I thought about my visions, the ones I had gotten at my baptism a while back. I had decided that the moons meant I should trust in Luna. Had I done that? I didn't know. I had always been worried, so maybe that meant that I hadn't.

The next image had been of...my father? It all made sense. He looked like Deverex, and...like me. And the image had turned into Deverex. Oh, great. My father also had a front row seat to my downfall, to my failure, through the moon.

I couldn't get over that. But, forcing myself to move on, I thought about the next vision, a disturbing vision. Deter with his heart pierced by the laser. I was done lying to myself. I had had a crush on him, sort of. And I know that this whole mess wasn't his fault, that he didn't mean any of this, because neither did I. But I just wished that I had never met him.

Inside myself I knew that the vision was showing me his death and even deeper inside me, I still wanted to save him.

I knew exactly what the last vision had meant. It had been of Artic. Luna, through this vision, had been trying to warn me, but I hadn't listened. Because I hadn't, Deverex was now dead. And the world was speeding down a slide that led to a pit of death.

Only now did I know what listening meant. I had never listened before. That's why Deverex, my brother, was dead. Why I was here. Why the world was hurling towards its end. And only now did I listen—to the utter despair of the earth itself. I wished I had listened to Luna. *I really, really wish I had listened,* I thought. Everything had happened so perfectly for the worst to happen now. I just wished I could fix it all right now. I knew I couldn't start over, so I didn't wish for that. What I wished for, in that dark room, looking up at Luna like a child looking at new toys, was something that I could do right now to fix everything. Something to help my brother and the world and the strength to do it, for I was a servant of Luna.

The moon seemed so close. It was strong, and mildly hypnotizing, like an ever-so-slight spice on your tongue. I felt bonded to Luna, how a servant feels bonded to his master. Finally, I felt strong, and I knew that Luna had heard my wishes and sincere sorrow. She was going to help me – help us both rather, as we had the same mission. In my hand was the laser!

CHAPTER XXX

The laser had magically ended up in my hands because of Luna! This was my shot at redemption, and Luna was giving it to me.

I knew I had to hurry, for maybe there was some way that I could resume the running of the waterfall. Perhaps I could be accepted as the Waterkeeper. I was the closest living thing to a Waterkeeper after all. Swiftly, for time was of the essence, I used the laser to cut my shackles, carefully, so as not to burn myself. I then clipped it to my necklace the same way I had the night I stole it.

I guess you could say that I had stolen the laser twice from Artic - once now and once before. Wait, that was it! How did Artic have the laser? He couldn't have gotten it from beyond the waterfall. Deverex was constantly checking on it—well, had been. You can't get through the hole unless the Waterkeeper water is present, like in me or on Awanata's face, so he couldn't have gotten in. Dr. Artic certainly didn't possess that water; that was a fact. Then the only way Artic could have had a laser...

With a big smile and hope for the first time in a while, I escaped the building, using the laser to cut through walls, and set on my way as fast as my legs could carry me.

It was hard to find the hole at night. However, I found another way to find it. *Run towards the moon and you'll find it*, came guidance from within. Clever Luna.

I had to run through town at one point. Even though it was after midnight, people and news reporters were running around everywhere, freaking out because everything was dying so quickly. I just ran past all of them, following the moon until I was far off.

As quickly as ever, I jumped in the hole, quickly passed it, and then got through the stone wall. The beauty everywhere was not lush and green and singing now – it was blue, and gray – mourning, moaning. I knew time was almost up.

The waterfall – it had stopped! It was now just a towering black wall – and nothing was behind it.

I rushed around the corner and took the path to the top of the waterfall, where the tall, wild grass usually flows in the wind.

I immediately rushed to the place where the never-ending stream of water meets the land. Had the waterfall really stopped? Could I fix it?

It was no use. I quickly spotted dry land on the top of the waterfall. That meant there was absolutely nothing I could do. It was dry. I was hopeless now. The end had come. I was too late.

Hopeless, I sat down on the cliff, dangling my feet out, and buried my face in my hands. As I wept, I noticed my foot was slightly damp. But certainly it couldn't be from my tears! I looked down and witnessed the biggest miracle since water itself; a trickle of water was flowing over my foot and down the falls! Looking around, I noticed another, and another!

This could only mean one thing: Deverex was still alive! As long as he was alive, some water would flow down the waterfall. However, I saw the signs, and knew that Deverex wouldn't live for much longer. I had to save him. And there was only one way to get there quickly enough – to jump down the waterfall.

I looked down. I was high up. I felt like I had been punched in the stomach. The pool of water at the bottom was still there, and I knew it was big, but from my vantage point, it looked like a speck. If I jumped down and hit land, I'd die in an instant. If I dove in at the wrong angle, I'd break my neck – and die then too. It reminded me of a documentary I once watched on birds that dove in the ocean for fish. In a huge flock, they lost about one bird per feeding time.

I didn't want to be the dead bird.

The only way to get down safely and quickly was to do it at the exact perfect angle. From this high up, it seemed impossible. Were my chances really that great?

The moon shone brighter all of a sudden.

I was a servant of Luna.

Without any further hesitation, I dove, aiming right for the reflection of the moon on the water below.

It was dark. My lungs felt oppressed, like some great weight was pushing in on them from all angles. The same feeling took over my head...and my whole body. I looked all around, from side to side and down. Everything was black. A deep, impenetrable black. So black that I felt like if I had looked at it too long, it would flood into me, which meant there was no escape because this black was everywhere. So I shut my eyelids, which did me absolutely no good because it was the same black. And then I wasn't sure when my eyelids were open or not, but I was pretty sure they were closed.

To make things worse, I discovered that it was hard to move. It took twice as much power just to bend my leg. All my limbs felt twice as heavy as usual.

Had I died when I dove down the waterfall? Did I dive into the pool wrong or miss it altogether? Was this my punishment for eternity because I had destroyed the world? To live in this unforgiving blackness forever, that seemed to be crushing me slowly?

The blackness seemed to be collapsing on me and my whole body felt so oppressed that I felt like I would explode at any moment. It only got worse, the torture, the pain—there seemed to be no escape! I didn't know if I could stand it for another second, much less spend my eternity like this. The torture! Oh, my regrets!

Suddenly, I became aware that I couldn't breathe. I couldn't breathe? I couldn't breathe! That meant that I had to breathe, that I was alive! I hadn't died, I had dived into the pool correctly!

The pool!

So was that where I was? In the pool below the waterfall? But why was it so dark? I must have been so far down that the light of the moon couldn't reach.

The moon! If the moon was up, then all I had to do was find it and swim to it, and eventually reach the surface. Then I could save Deverex! I could save the world after all!

If I could get there in time.

I started swimming in the direction of the only light: up. I had to draw energy from some unknown reservoir within me, although I'm not sure if that unknown reservoir even existed. Somehow I swam and the light kept getting brighter and brighter!

My lungs were collapsing more and more every second and I wasn't sure if I would make it to the surface in time, but the light was right there...

Suddenly, *pop*!

For a few seconds I wasn't sure if my lungs had actually popped or I had reached the surface. Then, I became aware that I was breathing very heavily, over and over, trying to gasp more air than I actually could. I had lived! As quickly as I could, I swam to the shore, and allowed one quick minute for myself to recover. Afterwards, I stood up, with at least a little bit of strength, and glanced at that great, wonderful, big moon – first it's reflection, then the real thing. And I knew if I tried, I'd get the job done. With that, I went off, with newfound strength.

CHAPTER XXXI

Retracing my steps was difficult with so much weighing on my mind.

With some difficulty, I found the odd, stone building, past town. I was about 100 yards from it when I froze.

Where would Deverex be in this weird building?

Well, he must be in the basement of the place, I thought. That's the only place where a freezer room – or whatever Deverex must've been in – could function properly, because it'd be cooler down there. Up above, it'd be too hot. If there are two things noticeable about Dry Cove, it's that it's hot and parched. A freezer would likely break down above ground in Dry Cove.

Very carefully, I carved a pinhole with the laser at the base of the building – which would be the high wall of the cellar. The pinhole was just big enough to see through.

The small room was dark, nothing there...

What's that? A small whining sound caught on the breeze. I listened more intently. There it was again – it was – a sob. A small, weak, helpless sob. I peeped through the hole again. This time, someone was in view, curled up in a ball, crying with his head in his hands.

It was Deter.

I felt bad for him. His life was really hard. So much hatred was ingrained in his family's past that it was almost as essential to their being as their blood or bones.

Everyone forced him to nurse that hatred inside himself, but he didn't have it. His mother and father were dead, so now he was with Artic, who gave him either sin or a ticket to jail. Luna had seemingly abandoned him. I felt a terrible strike of compassion, but I mean, he wasn't the only one with pain. I had no father, a dying brother, and had just destroyed the world.

I then realized that we had the same problem. We both wanted a different path than what could be taken. When we tried to make a path, it blew up in our faces. But this was how the world was – cruel, heartless, and cold.

I had to leave though, and ignore that painful streak of understanding. For I had a job to do and I wasn't giving up.

I turned 'round the corner and made another peep-hole, and a rush of cold air came at my eye while peeking in. Huge hope lifted my heart. I had arrived at the right place.

After proceeding to cut a hole big enough for me to slip through, I swiftly yet cautiously entered the building. The room indeed was a big, giant freezer. And there, in the center, was Deverex. There my beautiful, godly, dying brother appeared before me – he was pure ice.

My dying brother—so many reasons why that tore and slashed at my insides. This block of ice used to be a breathing, living, feeling, person that I loved. Of course, I loved my mother, and Awanata, and many other people, but I had loved Deverex more than all of them. Deverex, well, he had given me new life. He had given me a chance to start over, and he had taught me so much. Sometimes he had taught me consciously, like when he showed me how to find the birds in the trees or how to calculate how close the moon was to the world, but other times, he taught me without knowing it. Like when he taught me to open up, or truly listen, or to *understand*, to feel sorry, to regret – to forgive.

My regret had never been stronger than right then, looking at my dying brother.

I missed him so much already. Being around him had always made me so happy. He was responsible and so much more. But he would never make me happy or laugh or teach me again.

Out loud, I started mourning. "Loyal, strong, responsible, respectful, smart, generous, caring, so – so selfless. Forgiving! So forgiving of me! A stupid, careless, unfeeling, misunderstanding sinner as me!"

It was true – all of it.

Deverex had been everything I strived to be. He possessed every virtue I tried to develop, and more. Much, much more. I wanted to be like him, and I found myself making an idol out of him. He had always been there for me, even after I was not there for him and had totally betrayed all of his trust.

And now he was gone. Just like Father, pretty much like Mother, just like…me. Mourning them, I actually forgot what hope was. I simply and completely forgot what it was. Memories of it faded away, and trying to remember what hope had ever felt like made me feel numb.

While tears blurred my vision, I pushed Deverex's statue into the light of the moon. If anything could melt him, wouldn't it be Luna? The laser was helpless by now. It would burn or vaporize Deverex, not gently melt him. I waited a few minutes with him there in the moonlight, but to my despair, he only got colder, putting him further away from this world every second.

Maybe the moonlight wasn't strong enough? Maybe he had to be put outside to melt in the heat naturally? With the laser, I cut a big hole in the wall so I had enough room to push him through and then get up myself. Carefully, as if laying his dead body on a bed, I took Deverex's small monument and leaned it against the building wall.

Now he had natural, outside heat and the light of Luna. If anything could save him, this combination was it. I would just have to hope that he would live, and turn back into the living brother that I loved.

Hope?

The building was isolated enough that at least I didn't have to worry about other people finding Deverex's body. Luna knows where Artic must have been at the time. Unfortunately, I knew where Deter was. These were the only things I knew about the outside world. All I could think about was Deverex. I loved him too much for this to be his end. Since he didn't have any children, and since I was not wholly a Waterkeeper, no one would be able to resume his position. The world would die in as awful a way as Deverex would. And I would be to blame.

For Deverex's life, I prayed. On my knees staring up at his face while tears ran down mine, I prayed to the moon.

I only knew one little official prayer, one that little kids recite before they go to bed. Grandmother had taught it to me. "Fold your hands, kneel down," she would say in her soft, gentle voice.

"Your light is a beacon,
Your presence a guide.
Stay with me, Queen Luna
Walk by my side."

Over and over I recited the words so that I didn't even realize I was saying them anymore. My tongue numbed and I automatically whispered the bundle of words, too many times to count. I hardly even knew I was talking anymore.

"Your light is a beacon,
Your presence a guide.
Stay with me, Queen Luna
Walk by my side."

Openly crying, I wailed between rhymes. Deverex was gone. His ice turned a dark blue and he was rock solid. The brother who had changed my life, who loved me enough to die for me even after I had betrayed him, was gone. His light had been a beacon, his presence a guide. He was no longer with me, no longer at my side. His light had been snuffed. He had died.

I stopped praying and stood up. My dirty hands caressed the ice of his face.

"Oh, Deverex," I grieved, "I'm so sorry. I loved you so much." No - that wasn't true. Even though he was dead, I didn't stop loving him. I would never stop loving him.

"No, I…I love you so much, Deverex. I'll always love you and I'll always be sorry. I just want you to be happy, because you never really were. Make the moon shine brighter. Before the world dies, in about three days, you better make the moon shine brighter, Deverex, to let me know you're okay. And I know that I'll never see you again. I'll be…thrown into the sun or worse, to live an eternal death. But I want you to know that I'm sorry. I failed the world, but worst of all, I failed you, Deverex."

"I'm sorry!" I wailed, and thrust my arms around his cold body. There, in the hot air of the night, crying loudly over Deverex, I grieved.

Grief is an incredibly heavy state. It makes one's whole body ache and feel like your lungs are about to pop. Some people grieve differently than others, and get over it differently than others too. Some would rather not think about it and surround themselves with happy distractions. Others just need someone to listen to their stories of sadness and woe. Others are a mixture of these, and more. I simply liked to cry, shedding one teardrop at a time, lightening my weight bit by bit. Usually I liked to dwell on my sadness until I could dwell on it with dry eyes. Once I got to that point, I tended to be near the end of the grieving process. Now I was simply crying, mourning over Deverex. Whenever I grieve, I think about how I'll never get over it, although because of time, I always do. However, this time I knew I would never recover because it simply would not be possible. My eternity would be grief itself, to punish me for the awful life I had lived.

Experiencing this cursed state, embracing what once was Deverex, I sobbed the "Grief Cry."

The Grief Cry is the most intense and painful part of the grieving process. I personally believe that everyone has one. It cannot be forced or skipped. Everyone has a different Grief Cry. For some it lasts for a short eternity, a dozen minutes or so, but for others it may last hours. For some it may come suddenly, the day of the death or the day after it. For others still, the Grief Cry dwells within them, unhatched until it is unleashed in an explosion weeks or years later. No Grief Cry is easier than another and every Grief Cry is the most painful one. When some people experience this interval of hell, their bodies rack uncontrollably or radiate such awfully sad vibes that anyone around them could cry at that moment too. Grief Cries truly are unavoidable, uncontrollable, and unbearable. They sometimes seem to cause more pain to the griever than what the person who died must have experienced. Witnessing someone suffer a Grief Cry is unbearably sad too. I'd only seen a few Grief Cries, yet all of them still haunt me.

I still remembered when my mother's dear brother-in-law went. I'd flown in from Dinta to be with her. I stayed about a week and then I had to leave her. It was the saddest, hardest thing all of it. And I witnessed her Grief Cry.

Never before had I felt so helpless. Her spasms shook the whole bed we were lying on, and nothing – nothing could soothe her just for those few minutes. Tears streamed down her face as rapidly as a waterfall. It was as if she was literally choking on grief. Her emitting sadness was so powerful it made me want to cry too. Those few, never-ending minutes of my mother's Grief Cry still haunted me sometimes. They would keep me awake at night. The worst part is that it's nearly impossible to forget a Grief Cry. It's permanently stuck in one's head.

Now it was my turn, and I was all alone. My body ached and racked so bad that I lost control of myself. I felt light-headed and tears poured down my cheeks. My lungs felt near collapse, just like they had in the bottom of the pool under the waterfall. But this time, the impenetrable black that I so feared would consume me started on the inside, and worked its way out. Grief choked me. *Please Luna. Just kill me now, I beg of you!*

Deverex was now so cold that he was burning. I was so overcome with sadness that I didn't think or move or anything. I just kept hugging him. My heart was so sad.

CHAPTER XXXII

When I could finally breathe again, the wind picked up. It ruffled my hair and shirt and whistled through the hole in the wall. It was a warm wind, but I still felt cold on the inside and didn't dare open my eyes.

Then the wind whistled again – the strangest whistle I've ever heard. Wait – it wasn't the wind...it was a voice, saying...

"Kyla."

My eyes bolted open and my heart started pounding so fast that it hurt. I got light-headed again. What? I never thought I'd hear that voice again...

I looked up.

"Deverex?"

It hadn't been the wind at all. Deverex hugged me back, ruffling my shirt and hair. My joy was so intense that I was dizzy and started crying all over again! My heart was still pounding and my legs felt weak.

"Deverex!" I shouted, embracing him harder. "You're alive! Oh my god, you're alive! I'm so happy, I don't know what to do! Deverex, you were dead! I tried to save you, but it was too late. Oh my god, Deverex, you're alive!" I laughed with tears of joy.

We just held each other for a long time. I was so joyful.

The brother that I loved with all my heart was simply alive and the world was not over because of me. I don't know how many times I thanked Luna in my head that night. I have thanked her every night, ever since.

"Oh my god, Deverex," I whispered with a shaky voice. "I love you so much."

"I love you too, Kyla."

"I never thought I'd hear that again."

I know what love is. I do. Because I felt it so strongly that night. And ever since, I have had a deeper understanding.

Deverex and I embraced each other for a while. We couldn't control our joy. However, as my tears began to dry, something else popped into my mind, and I couldn't ignore it.

Deter.

"Deverex, Deter!" I said, standing up. "We have to find him, and we have to get out of here!"

"What?" he asked, totally taken by surprise. "Wait, who's Deter and who cares? We have to get out of here," he finished, quite determined. "I let time slip away. I forgot that we're still in a dangerous place!"

"No," I said stepping in front of him and blocking his way.

"Deter is Artic's grandson," I said. "But we have to save him. We have to find him and get out of here! He needs us Deverex, he needs freedom, and he needs love!" I whispered, still standing, strong and determined myself.

Deverex stared straight into me. "Are you out of

your mind? He's an Artic, his family is sin itself. Boy, he needs…a lot of things, but love from us, is *not* one of them. Look Kyla, I was just so happy to be alive that I forgot that Artic is still very near. We're still in grave danger and I need to get back to the waterfall!" he said, strong enough that the average person would've backed off. But not me.

"No!" I screamed, "*No!* He does need a lot of things, including love from us. He needs a second chance – forgiveness. Deverex, you gave me a second chance didn't you? When I betrayed you, you forgave me. Now you have to forgive him. Was he the very man that attempted to kill the Waterkeeper 3,915 years ago? No, he wasn't! He's just unluckily—and not by choice by the way—related to that man. He wouldn't kill you if it meant that he could revive his dead mother. He wouldn't kill you if it meant that he could *be* the Waterkeeper! I've met him Deverex, and he's only shown me kindness. Don't roll your eyes like that! He could've killed me if he wanted to but he didn't. If the First Ones are a family of love, then why aren't you showing it to him? Trust me. I was wrong when we fought, but I know now that most people haven't changed. But I'm right in that some people have. You broke tradition yourself Deverex. You let me in. Maybe Deter's breaking his own family traditions too. I love you, Deverex and I won't put you in harm's way again. Trust me. Please. Let us save Deter."

Silence.

He wouldn't look at me now; he just stared at the ground and sighed.

"Okay," he whispered weakly. "Let's go save him."

"Oh my gosh, thank you Deverex, you won't regret this! Hurry, this way, we don't have much time."

"You got that right!" Deverex said, trailing behind.

"I suspect we won't need to worry about the ice gun. I saw it in the room that you were frozen in. Artic won't…"

"Why didn't you take the gun?!"

"What if I had misfired it? It's too dangerous and too big to carry around. We have no need for it anyway. But we don't need to worry about it because Artic thinks he doesn't need it now, so he won't have it. Besides, he thinks you're in there and he doesn't want to unlock the door to get it. He thinks the risk is too big."

"Well then, why didn't you at least destroy it?"

"Oh. Sorry. I didn't have time, or even think of that. But anyway, the laser – trust me, we don't need to worry about that at all."

Deter wasn't in that room where I had seen him, which alarmed me. Then I would have to go into this cursed building to find him…

"Can we enter the building through some door in the ice room?" Deverex asked.

"No," I said. "I have a suspicion that Artic won't be too far from there." I suddenly realized that Deverex couldn't come with me to save Deter. This was meant for me. He had to tend to the waterfall anyway. He had already skimmed death once, he didn't need to plunge into it now. If I died trying to save Deter, I'd be in peace because Deverex was alive.

But I had to try.

"Deverex, you need to get back. Go look after the waterfall. I need to do this alone."

He was taken aback. "What!? I'm sorry, I'm confused..."

"Deverex...please."

Again silence.

"Kyla don't go spending your life for a stranger that you met once, that's so crazy."

"Please Deverex, this isn't about me! This isn't even about you. It's so much more than that, but you need to go, please trust me."

Deverex looked completely frustrated, but he knew he wouldn't win. "Alright, but...be careful okay?"

A hug. A farewell. Then I turned around the next corner of the building as Deverex turned into water form and trickled away.

I bored another peephole using the laser. This revealed an empty chamber similar to the one I was in earlier. More uncharted territory, but I didn't know what else I would find if I kept circling the building, so I slipped in and hid in a corner.

Two minutes passed and nothing came through the doorway, so I figured the hallway, or whatever it was outside, was in the clear. Fear filled me again and wrestled with my determination and I waited just one more minute to see which side of myself would win the fight. Actually, I didn't have much control over what I was doing now really, but suddenly I was out in the hallway.

The hallway looked basically the same as all the eerie chambers in the building-unkempt, dusty stone.

Surprised by myself, I had the laser up and ready for use in front of me if needed. A few more steps revealed another chamber room to me, on my left. It was empty, just like the next three that I passed. I was so terrified that I could feel my heartbeat in my stomach and my head was throbbing. Every too-powerful heartbeat sent fluttering yellow and blue dots into my vision.

I wondered what would be worse—dying of heart failure or by some gunshot wound Artic would inflict on me. Neither alternative seemed ideal, but both seemed awfully likely.

I passed a fourth chamber, then a fifth.

And then the weeping again—his weeping, coming from the sixth room.

He wasn't dangerous and I knew it. But my first glance of Deter surrounded by weapons made me question my first feelings of him.

His back was to me and all I could hear was a mixture of sad, raging, and vengeful mumbles. He hadn't noticed me yet when I noticed what he was doing. Deter was taking apart and mutilating exotic weapons on the table. He was dismantling them. Breaking them.

Now he picked up a shiny gun at least two feet long and awfully bulky. His facial expression, visible in the reflection of the gun, changed from concentration to rage to fear and back again, all in a second.

Then our eyes met in the reflection.

For a second, time stopped and I didn't know why I still felt a hint of fear. Then he turned around and looked into my eyes.

Time stopped again. His face changed from fear to softness and I finally saw again that kind boy in the woods of Dry Cove.

"So what's the quickest route out of this cursed prison?" he asked in a barely audible voice.

Deter couldn't quite believe what I had just risked to save him, but I knew exactly what was happening. Now I had to hope that Luna would give me a safe route out of the small building, which I was nearly certain used to be a small jail.

Once again I was scared because of one thing: Artic.

I figured just going out the way I had come was safest. Halfway back, I started to wonder if Deter was seeing yellow and blue dots too, and it occurred to me that I actually could be dreaming or even dead. The pain in my head and chest ruled that idea out, which for some reason disappointed me. I couldn't feel my legs, but thought I knew fairly certainly that they were the things moving me. Behind my eyes, the area where my thoughts formed, seemed hot and the thoughts seemed tangled. My chest couldn't seem to grab much-needed air and was that thumping from Deter's footsteps or my head? *But just keep going*, I told myself, *you're halfway there, three-quarters of the way out, almost free...*

Suddenly, I realized that the thumping was definitely not me and I didn't think it was coming from Deter either. *No*, I realized, *it's further away.*

Deter stopped suddenly – he must have heard it too. I turned around to look at him. Fear ruled inside and out of him obviously, but I must have looked the exact same way. Deter and I continued down the corridor of hell without a sound. The thumping didn't stop.

Then, the most horrible feeling ran through me. It felt like there wasn't enough blood in my body and I couldn't swallow. It was the worst sensation of fear that I had ever felt. I felt like I could very easily collapse and die right then if I didn't keep myself moving.

Deter and I turned one blind corner away from freedom, when I heard the blood curdling,

"Kyla Marine, why do you dare to entertain me?"

He stood right in front of me. My only exit was twenty yards away, and Artic stood blocking it.

He was wild. His face was that of the devil, and there was fire in his eyes. His body movements were similar to that of a monster. He was a monster. The crevices of his face were lined by shadows and his eyes bore into his head.

It was as if his body was a reflection of his soul, and I couldn't rip my eyes away.

He let the sight of the monster he had become sink in, and then he laughed a sound that made me feel like he was sucking out my soul.

"All my family's life, there was only one goal. That was to end the Waterkeeper's reign. My son, myself, my father before me, his father before him! There was always only one point to living and that was to kill—to kill the Water-keeper. All of us; we breathed to stop him from breathing. And every. Single. Generation. Failed."

Somehow, for some reason, I felt two people inside of me. One wanted to flail her arms in front of her and make all of this vaporize into nothing, and be back in Dinta, pretending this nightmare never happened. The other was strong. She was not afraid, but steady, ready. She knew what she had to do and was prepared to do it. She understood.

"We've come close though. So very close. Way back 3,915 years ago, we almost succeeded. Tonight, tonight I almost succeeded. But I see you now and I know the truth. I will never succeed."

At this he smiled and laughed, but it was as if he was dying.

I could still feel both people within me. Once of them forced me to look away, and the other continued looking to confirm a suspicion; she was right.

It was so carefully hidden—low on the wall, at my leg. Untrained eyes would never have found it.

A door.

"It is that simple. Victory is impossible. Happiness is impossible. Meaning. Is. Impossible."

"So why then, am I living? I am indeed not living but am merely alive. My family has wasted everything, has wasted life itself, *we* are waste. And it's just not fair. Your name is praised, our name is cursed. And no matter what my family tried, we could never change a thing. We had no importance, no power, no effect. And it took us this long to realize it. Too late," Dr. Artic continued.

I was now aware, staring at the door, that the laser was clipped to my necklace. I'd forgotten I put it there. Dr. Artic didn't know I had it.

Slowly, I slipped my hand behind my back and motioned toward the door. I knew Deter wouldn't be able to see it, but as long as he was looking in that direction...

"We failed, Kyla. Do you know what it's like to fail? I don't believe you do. So let me show you. You failed to make it out of this dungeon alive. Burn in hell! Then you'll know what it's like to fail!"

With that, he pulled the laser out from his back and pointed it at my forehead.

The two people inside of me were trying to shout over each other, so my head filled and I couldn't hear a thing.

With one incredibly swift movement, I kicked the door and opened it. Deter didn't need to be given directions, he was through it and gone within a moment. I realized I had to do something too, but what?

Here was the moment that fulfilled the prophecies. The decision of the century. The future of the world and goodness itself. This was it. Within me. I could either flee and escape the evil testing me, or I could...

But could I?

No one would ever be able to blame me if I ran away. No one would ever be able to judge my decision, because they wouldn't understand that feeling of terror pushing on your lungs and heart and head. The feeling that wakes you in the night, unable to feel any part of your body. They wouldn't be able to blame me because of that feeling that makes your blood run cold at one hundred miles per hour and makes your heart pound at the speed of light. No one would ever understand the moment where your body feels frozen, except your heart, which is a caged rocket that needs to go somewhere.

No one would ever know the truth.

The world had waited 3,915 years.

This was not only the world's second chance, but it was mine—again. I had had so many second chances, and for that I was grateful. What was I to do now?

"We're actually not that different, you and I," I said, gesturing for him to wait. "But here's one difference: you don't believe in anything. I believe in everything."

With one swipe, my necklace snapped and the laser was pointed at his heart.

This was the prophecy. I was a servant of Luna.

CHAPTER XXXIII

Artic lay on the ground in a pool of dark blood, motionless at my feet. Those eyes were staring straight back into mine. I thought about all of those times back in Dinta's prestigious little school, where he had stared down into me. *That won't be happening again*, said the voice that had won inside my head.

I stooped down beside Artic. This man had been born to hate. Had been raised to kill. He had never known what love is. All his life the evil had grown inside him like a parasite. It had sucked everything else out of him until nothing else remained, so he had become a mindless monster. Bad things happen when love is not there—very bad things.

Now, crouching beside his dead body, I realized something: even though all his life he had said that he wanted revenge, and had worked towards it, I don't think that he ever knew what he really wanted. Maybe that's what had happened, and he really had been just a cranky, sad old man.

I guessed that's how I thought we were similar. Back in Dinta, neither of us had known what we had wanted, what we had needed. Back in Dinta, neither of us had been living, but had been merely alive. Since then, one thing was different: I knew what I wanted, and I already had it all back at the waterfall.

Looking back at it all now, back at his dead body, I knew that none of it mattered anymore.

The prophecies had been fulfilled.

For some unknown reason, my hand gently touched his body and it lingered over his still, silent lungs.

Suddenly, I jumped away from his body as I realized with surprise that it was crumbling like rocks on a slope. First the face, then the fingers, and then the rest. As he was crumbling, air was smoldering out of him with a horrific screaming sound.

I covered my ears with my palms but the piercing scream only grew louder. It was as if all the horror and terror that had been trapped inside the Artics since the Second One was letting go. I felt my eyeballs vibrate in their sockets and my headache was as bad as the time I had fallen off the waterfall.

The scream continued as I collapsed on the ground, coughing on suffocating screams that were centuries old.

I closed my eyes and when I opened them again after who knows how long, everything was completely silent. It was as if time was frozen, it was that silent. For a second I believed that I was deaf before I heard myself coughing again.

When I recovered I saw what lay on the floor: a pile of dust.

And a laser.

I picked it up and weighed it in my hand. *Just as I thought.*

CHAPTER XXXIV

The dawn was blinding. Sunrays wrapped themselves around me and sank into my veins, becoming liquid gold. The sun hit upon my face as the wind trickled through my hair. The whole sky was a pure orange-pink color, as if the world was enclosed in a loving heart. On the horizon the sun was a milky fountain of justice, leaking light and letting it run down and absorb the world.

Examining everything, I saw that no trees were dying, no flowers were wrinkling up, brown. Everything was alive and thriving, including the people of Dry Cove. Dry Cove was still dry, but instead of being lifeless like it had been before, it was vibrant. It was filled with movement. Instead of being infested with shadows, it was tinted by a flawless, heavenly light from the dawn.

It was beautiful.

But I had been spoiled; I'd seen a much more beautiful sight, which I needed to go back to.

I knew Deverex would be at the hole, probably with Deter, waiting for me. I didn't believe that Deverex would do any harm to Deter, but he would look at him with un-trusting eyes. He was probably worried out of his mind for me, my brother, but he would have to wait.

I walked slowly back to the hole, back to the door to home, because I lingered a while, breathing in the magical sunlight. I lingered while taking in this new world, bathed in solar bliss. It would never be the same as the one I used to know.

The prophecies had been fulfilled.

I lingered while taking in something else that would never be the same as the one I used to know: myself. Now I wasn't a meaningless, unhappy, scared shadow. I was the Prophecy. I understood the Truth and I was happy, not scared anymore. I never would be again.

And in that moment, walking in the sacred sunlight, I laughed as I told myself that I was still plenty stubborn.

Deverex embraced me and held me tight for a long time. A few hours ago, I had thought I would never feel this again, so even though the hug hurt a little, I hugged him back tightly. After a long time he retreated and stared me straight in the eye.

"I want you to know that I'm never forgiving you."

Immediately I was frozen and my breath fled me. Tears filled my eyes faster than I could stop them or blink them away, so when I tried to blink the tears ran down my cheeks and soon I was sobbing.

"Deverex, I'm so sorry. I didn't mean to be afraid so you would come and save me, I didn't know that you would come! Artic had the laser to my head, and I was scared for my life! I'm so sorry he froze you because of me. I didn't know when I told Deter I followed Luna that Luna's Way was illegal, I didn't know anything then; I didn't mean to tell him. I didn't mean to give you away or put your life in jeopardy. It would have been best if I hadn't been born, that wouldn't have happened. Deverex, I'm sorry, I love you…"

Above me, Deverex whispered, "What?"

I stood up, wiping my nose. "I didn't mean to tell Deter when I met him in Dry Cove before I knew you, that I followed Luna's Way. I didn't know that The First and Second Ones are her only followers. I didn't know anything then. If I hadn't said that then, Artic wouldn't have known we were related, he wouldn't have used me to try to kill you. I'm sorry. I tried to repent by saving you, but if that didn't work, then I don't think there's anything I can do but say that I'm sorry and I love you."

Deverex looked confused, then he sighed and closed his eyes, saying, "Oh Kyla, you think it's all your fault. It wasn't. Are you listening? It wasn't Kyla, it wasn't your fault. It wasn't anyone's fault. And it's fine now. You did it, Kyla. You saved me."

Now I was starting to cry again as I embraced my brother, whom I loved with all my heart. After a minute I asked, "So what are you mad at me for then?"

"Because you took so long to come back after I left you at the jail. I was waiting here forever. You don't know that feeling Kyla, what it's like to leave someone you love alone to face the biggest danger there ever was. And they don't come back and you think they never will. And there's nothing you can do because you were stupid and failed to protect them."

I stared down at my hand. "I think I do know that feeling, Deverex." I said quietly. "I felt it right before you were shot with ice."

Deverex was taken aback, realizing I was right. Then

he was frustrated with me and he huffed out a quick breath of exasperation. A fist shot out and hit my left arm. I let out a small whine and grabbed my arm. It hurt. But he got shoved backwards in return, his face showing emotions like hurt, anger, relief, and brotherly revenge all at the same time. But before the fight continued, I gave my big brother a hug, and he returned the hug instead of another punch.

CHAPTER XXXV

"So, where's Deter?" Deverex asked expectantly.

I had a headache again. "What? He's not with you?"

"Kyla, that's not funny."

"What? No! I thought you had taken him back to the waterfall or something, he should've gotten out—"

"Why would I leave *him* alone at the waterfall? Hold on, gotten out of what?"

"Out of the tunnel. We were facing Artic and he had to—"

"You faced Artic?"

"Yeah, I'm okay, I'll tell you about it later. So Deter had to escape and I found a door and...Deverex!"

"What happened, where is he now, are you all right? How did you—"

"Deverex, I'm fine, don't worry about it right now. We need to find Deter first!" I huffed. His wide eyes and distracted questions were getting on my nerves.

"So we were facing Artic," Deverex blinked several times at that, "and he had to escape so I found one of the doors. I kicked it open and he went through it. Do you know where the tunnel from the old prison leads? He should be at the end of it by now, that was...a while ago."

Still a little distracted, Deverex subconsciously scratched the back of his neck. "Oh that one? I think that leads, um..."Deverex thought a moment, working through tunnel intersections and exits and side tunnels in his head.

Suddenly, he stood up tall and stared straight ahead.

"Do you really believe that Deter's good?" he asked, now staring at me.

"I do," I said with confidence. I didn't know what this had to do with anything.

"If he's not, then he's already dead in the hole, but if he is, there's a chance that both the First and Second Ones can get through if they are truly good inside. He might be at the—"

I never did hear that last word. Deverex was already gone, into the hole, and I was right behind him.

We raced past the forest of the enchanted green. The moment was exciting, although anxious as well and even though I was focused, I couldn't help but smile at the green all around. Last night I had thought this place would never be green again. Now, here it was, my favorite shade of green.

The Grand Hall opened in front of Deverex and me. It hadn't stopped opening by the time we were through.

Here it was, this beautiful paradise, right in front of my eyes. It still shook something in me every time I entered.

Although I was far from the waterfall, its vibrations still shook the ground. I could hear the birdsong that filled the silence. It sounded different than before. The massive weeping willow, which I had come to know as the Mother Tree, swayed in the wind, as if there was a child between its branches that it was rocking to sleep.

The water was crystal clear, and pure. The breeze came by to tinkle all of the natural wind chimes.

I realized something. This place always shook me when I entered, but before now, something else had stirred inside me too. I had never before come close to placing it. I believe it had been the feeling that something wasn't quite right. Even in paradise, something had kept it from being perfect. It had been the feeling of everything holding its breath. The place hadn't been still, obviously, and the birds had still sung, but everything had been waiting for something. It had been waiting in the empty pockets of the air that were hard to notice because lots of the time, something else hid them so well.

Now nothing was waiting anymore. Now those empty, elusive pockets were full, and paradise itself was exhaling into gorgeous laughter. Now the Night had gone, and Day was flowering. I saw it. I heard it. I was there.

A verse kept repeating in my head:
"I have seen the Glory of the Sunrise;
I have felt the warmth of the Sun;
I have heard the Victory of the Birdsong;
I have seen the Goodness of a New Day."
I have seen the Goodness of a New Day.

Deverex watched him from a few feet behind. There he was, kneeling at the waterside, just like someone else had done under the Mother Tree. I was relieved to see him, even though I knew he'd be here. I ran up beside him and Deverex followed.

He turned to me. With red eyes and a soft yet sturdy voice, Deter asked, "What is this place?"

I turned to Deverex. He was whispering to himself. "I was wrong Luna, he really is good."

The first place I took Deter to was the top of the waterfall. For a long time he just sat there and stared at everything.

I sat beside him.

The sun went down some behind us to the right before I asked, "Why did they name you Determine?"

Deter didn't respond. I thought he had ignored me and moved on silently, but after a moment, he told me:

"I was to determine my family's fate."

I looked at him.

"Not once did any of them ever look at me as if they were satisfied with me. Never once. Except my mother. She told me she loved me. She told me that I had to find who I was, to not let other people tell me who to be. When I was little I didn't understand. They started calling me Deter because I was supposed to deter the Waterkeeper's eternal reign from happening. But instead, I deterred the outcome that my family always wanted."

"You did. That must've taken a lot of courage sometimes," I pondered.

Deter let out a small sound, which sounded something like a cross between a sigh and a laugh.

"It was a little hard feeling like I didn't belong in my own family. If you don't belong there, where will you belong?"

I looked at him again from where I had shifted my gaze to the waterfall. "You didn't belong."

He returned my gaze.

"You never were an Artic. Not really, not at all. You were something different all along. They were never your family besides your mother. You should never think of yourself as an Artic again because, you never were one, and now you've proven that because you're sitting where you are now."

"Who's my family now?"

"Us."

Deter paused and stared back out at the golden-tipped trees. So did I.

What a shade of green, I mused.

"What type of family?" he asked.

I paused and said, "I don't know."

He looked at me and then I looked back into his eyes right next to me.

"What about this type?" he whispered, and then he kissed me above the gushing waterfall.

Immediately my heart was rapidly beating inside my chest. It had been beating faster a lot lately, but this was different than any of the other times. Those times, I had been frightened. This time, I was exhilarated, happy, not afraid for my life or my brother's. I was filled with and excited for life instead. I hadn't felt this type of thrill before, and I loved it.

I think Deter did too.

The powerful rushing under us was proof that Deverex was strong inside. We sat there silently admiring it.

CHAPTER XXXVI

Dinner was served on the table. Deverex and Deter sat across from each other and I sat in the middle. There hadn't even been a conversation yet. We were all awkward and quiet.

I caught Deverex curiously looking at Deter, and I slapped him on the arm to make him stop.

The silence was too much. I decided to ask a question that had been lingering in my mind for a while to break it.

"I don't understand why Artic had an empty laser."

Both of them dropped their forks at the same time and looked at me with surprise.

"What?!" Deverex asked loudly.

His outburst startled me. Didn't he know? Oh, that's right, I hadn't told him about my last encounter with Artic yet. Or the empty laser.

"Oh, I haven't even told you yet. After I found Deter, we were almost out and then Artic was at the exit. So I found a door and sent Deter through it..."

"Why didn't you go yourself?" Deverex asked.

"Because I had already figured out the laser situation."

"Which was...." implored Deverex.

"I knew that Artic had a fake one." Deter's eyes widened at this, but he stayed quiet. "I had the real one. Before I escaped the prison when you were frozen, Luna gave me the laser that I stole from Artic's safe." Deter was surprised again. "So I knew that Artic's laser wasn't real. Artic threatened me with it…"

In a less serious moment, I could have laughed at their suspense.

"…and I killed him with mine."

Deverex was blinking as if I was blinding him and Deter was completely frozen. After a few silent moments, they both exclaimed in unison:

"*What?!*"

I smiled at the ground. "I did."

"And then what?" Deter whispered in a low voice.

I gazed at him. "I can't explain what happened next. I touched the body, and it began crumbling into dust. And seething out of it came this piercing scream." I shuddered remembering it. "I actually passed out at that point."

"When I came to, there was a pile of dust on the floor, and a laser. I opened it and it was empty, and…"

"What?" breathed Deter.

"I put his ashes in it."

I glanced at both of them. They were so surprised that it seemed like they didn't know what to do or feel.

"Where is it?" Deverex mumbled, barely breathing, he was so shocked.

"I put both lasers under the moon."

"In the chapel?"

"No, in the Moon Room. On that shelf under 3,915."

No one had eaten anything since I started talking, which reminded me of my first question.

"Do you know why it was a fake laser?" I said to Deter.

"I thought it was just Luna's magic."

It took him a minute to respond.

"I did it," he confessed. "I opened the vault one day and it wasn't there, so I made a fake without Artic knowing, thinking he couldn't hurt anyone with a false laser."

"Nice," Deverex whispered.

Deter looked up and smiled.

"Weren't you concerned where the real laser went?" I asked.

"I guess I should have been more concerned than I was. I just knew that anyone was better than him having it."

"Wait," Deverex ordered, his brow lowering. "Did Artic ever find out that it was a fake laser?"

"No, I – I mean, I don't think so." Deter replied. "Maybe besides right before Kyla killed him."

The words *Kyla killed him* echoed inside my head. I knew I shouldn't feel guilty about killing him, but I couldn't help it. *Kyla killed him. Kyla Marine killed someone. Someone who once breathed and lived, who once was an innocent child.*

Was he ever innocent? I didn't know.

I pictured a baby crying. An infant. Then, in my vision, I saw my own hand and in it was a laser...

Something touched my arm and I gasped and jumped in my chair. I looked up to see that it was Deverex trying to comfort me. Or maybe he was just trying to get my attention.

"Kyla, you shouldn't feel guilty. You did what had to

be done," Deverex told me, knowing exactly what I was thinking.

I hummed my agreement. He rubbed my arm and then continued his conversation with Deter.

"So if Artic didn't know that the laser was fake, what made him use an ice gun instead?" he interrogated.

"We thought..."

"*They* thought," I interrupted Deter. By continuing to identify with his family, he was stopping himself from letting go of his shame. Deverex glanced at me and back to Deter.

"They thought that ice represented them, in lots of ways. What once had been Holy Water now wasn't, symbolizing us...uh, well...them as the Second Ones. It represents in lots of other ways too. And he wanted you to die with the same ice he had felt his whole life," Deter explained. "He thought that nothing could un-freeze you."

"What about heat?" Deverex retorted.

Deter inhaled through his teeth. "This ice was different. It was based on hatred rather than cold. He didn't realize love would melt it."

"He didn't ever realize love," I summed up.

"Yeah."

"Hey," I started, "what about that crack in your ice statue?"

Deverex turned to me and his head lowered with his voice. "It's a scar."

"What!?"

"From my left hip to my right shoulder," he whispered,

stretching his shirt collar to show the beginning of it. His face was sad and full of pain. "It hurts."

I looked at Deter. He was coiled up, shutting down. I knew why.

"I handed him the gun," he breathed.

I sighed. "Deter, that wasn't your fault. It wasn't! You didn't even really give it to him, he would've just gotten the gun himself."

"I'm sorry," he remorsed to Deverex.

I saw Deverex look down with a hard brow. I, of all people, knew he was capable of holding a grudge for a while. Well, maybe that had been me more than him, but still…

His brow was hard, but slowly it softened. "It's all right," he mumbled. "Don't blame yourself."

Deter looked up, "Really?" He said, as if he were out of breath.

"Yes."

They looked at each other. Slowly, Deverex smiled a wide smile. Deter's face displayed an emotion I had only seen once before, when he first saw me in the prison.

It was hope.

Deverex and I sat outside, legs dangling in the water, near the waterfall, still close enough to the great pounding that the current pulled our legs sideways. Deter was in the Chapel. When he had been shown the room, it had been as if he'd shut down somewhat. He'd gotten quieter than normal and had acted as if he didn't trust the room. Yet he had wanted to spend some time in there anyway.

"So what about my life back in Dinta?"

Deverex gave me a queer, sideways look.

"I mean, how do I go back? *Do* I go back?"

"Of course you go back. You need an education and you can't just disappear. As far away as it may seem, you were there, what, two days ago, yesterday?"

"True."

"It'll never be the same as it used to be..."

"I know that."

Deverex laughed.

"What?" I said, not hiding the tinges of annoyance and defiance in my voice.

"A few months ago, you would've snapped, 'What do you know?' Now you're snapping, 'I already knew that.'"

I tried to scowl at Deverex, yet was smirking at the same time. I grabbed his arm and threatened to push him in the water with a light push.

Deverex laughed even harder.

"You know that wouldn't affect me."

"Whatever."

Now he was roaring. I was trying to calculate how I could get him back when he calmed down and stated, "No, seriously. We'll just make some story on how he died and let it leak out to the press. Dinta gets a new Head Master, everyone's safe and sound back in Dinta, including you, whoop-dee-do. Everything's okay."

Now it was my turn to laugh. "A few months ago, you would have never been so laid back about planning dinner tomorrow!"

He frowned at me, and then a smile formed on his face. I barely had time to see it before I was in the water – clothes and all.

Deverex burst out laughing. "It sure affects *you*, doesn't it?! Ha ha ha…!"

"Joke's on you," I taunted. "Water feels great!" I expressed this with a beautiful backstroke.

"Your hair looks frightfully horrid wet. And dry too, actually." Deverex advised.

"Like you're one to give advice on that! So will you come and visit in Dinta?"

Deverex looked confused and blinked a few times. "Well," he sighed, "What do you mean? Of course not. You'll just come and visit here like usual."

I was shocked a little. "You still don't get it?" I questioned. "After all that just happened? Deverex, the reason that I brought Awanata here was because you were so sad, not being able to see the world outside that wall." I pointed to the great stone barrier. "I wanted to save you from being trapped like that. I thought I could bring someone out there to you before bringing you out there. The Artics are gone! You don't need to fear them anymore, Deverex. Sure, you can never live outside in the world the way I can. But, come on! If you can't be part of it, then you can at least be in it. You're the only one holding you back now."

Deverex stared at me wide-eyed as if I was a ghost. I was starting to wonder how he could go so long without blinking when he finally looked away at the ground.

I swam up to him and held onto his ankles. He turned away more. His expression was either extreme longing or intense concern. I couldn't tell which. Well, maybe I could.

He held his breath like he was about to say something. He looked into my eyes, but then sighed and turned away. He was about to say something again but once more sighed.

Finally, he softly spoke, as if with some uncertainty.

"Maybe it would be all right." He looked up into my eyes and smiled. Both of our insides soared. I climbed out of the pool while he started a conversation. "So what did it feel like in that cell when I was frozen?"

I was a little surprised, but couldn't blame him for being curious. I had some questions too. So I told him.

"It was hell. To watch the world around you start to wither and die and you think it's all your fault. It's incomprehensible guilt. I told myself that I had to watch it. I told myself that I couldn't die because I didn't deserve relief."

He didn't say anything. I guess he got his answer. So I let myself ask my question.

"What was it like to be frozen?" I asked.

He hesitated, thinking back, and then revealed, "It was dark. My lungs felt oppressed, like some great weight was pushing in on them from all angles. The same feeling took over my head...and eventually my whole body. I looked all around, from side to side and down. Everything was black. A deep, impenetrable black. So black that you felt like if you looked at it too long, it'd flood into you. Which meant there was no escape, because black was everywhere."

Now the Light had replaced it.

My eyes darted open. All of a sudden, I was wide awake. I looked around the living room, where I was sleeping because Deter had the spare room. The room was flooded in an eerie white-blue light from the entrance by the waterfall.

It was like a dream in the sense that I knew exactly what was happening, even though I hadn't been told in any way. But it wasn't a dream. I was so awake. It was so real.

I got up and moved toward the entrance to the pool, as if hypnotized. I had been hypnotized and acted like this before, but my mind wasn't off this time: no, I was quite conscious, just knowing, determined, and willing.

I withdrew the pouring water like a curtain and stepped outside.

The great pounding muffled my head. The whole night was that same blue-white, the waterfall was painted silver. I stared, eyes locked, at the reflection of the moon in the pool. So many things had changed, but that mirror had stayed the same. I admired its beauty; there was nothing quite like it. Then I looked up at the real moon. Its light had opened the gates of my heart and now my heart was rushing like the Clear Waterfall itself.

EPILOGUE

The first time I ever took Deverex outside of his little world, he acted really weird. Most of what I showed him was places that he'd only ever seen at night before. He asked so many questions and then would be silent, deep in thought for a long time. Sometimes he would flinch at things, and once he nearly turned into his water form and jumped into the waterway before I calmed him. It was his first time truly free; he didn't know what to do with himself.

Yet part of his old self was still there. When he saw a temple to a god, he was outraged. I reminded him that the idol's worshippers were innocent and under the government's influence. He sighed through his teeth. When he met Awanata, posing as my friend, he acted really strange. She was the first girl from the outside that he had ever met. I ignored it at the time, thinking that he was simply out of his comfort zone, but the way that he looked at her...

She was always the prettier one of the two of us.

And I'll never forget when he first met our mother. I brought him along the next time I visited her. "I'm bringing a good friend," I'd said to her on the phone.

I made sure to watch his face when we came out of the tunnel from the plane. (Of course he wasn't staying the weekend, just the day and going back in the tunnels.)

Now, while my mother loved me and was always happy to see me, she wasn't really the supportive, hugging, loving type and was always trying to teach me how to behave. But she did embrace me when she saw me, so he knew who my mother was out of the many at the airport. I made sure to watch his face. You can imagine what it looked like.

And after being introduced to him, my mother said, "You two have strikingly similar blue eyes."

That was years ago. Since then, I have completed my education at Dinta. I have traveled to many different places, but found there is no place quite like home.

Awanata and I have restored our soul-sister bond. In fact, it is stronger now than it ever was in Dinta. She and Deverex have gone on an important journey – with each other. They fell in love and were married many moons ago. And no, the secret was not kept from Awanata. She lives in the paradise, in fact. She goes in and out by way of the hole in the newly restored forest in Dry Cove. What she does is drinks some water from the Waterfall, and that allows her to get back in within three days.

She and Deverex waited some years before having children – they knew that Deverex only had exactly thirteen years to live as soon as their first son was born. But their son is now nearly seven years old. He is a beautiful child. His smile triggers something within. I know he is destined for great things. He is destined to smile like that forever.

He's not the only one, of course; his little brother just

had his third birthday last month. His innocence is just what his aunt needs sometimes to still her.

I myself found love as well. I realized one evening that even the beautiful world itself is more beautiful when Determine is in it. We were married in a small ceremony, just us, Luna, Deverex, and Awanata. I need Determine to fill empty spaces within me. Just like the air on the morning after the legendary night of Artic's death, he fills empty spaces that I didn't know I have. I need his mellow kindness to keep my outgoing, somewhat defiant, stubborn self in check.

He lives at the Waterfall too, along with our son and daughter. My precious daughter is nine years old. She is surprisingly very studious, cautious, and alert. She is basically all of the good things I wasn't as a child. We are similar though, in that we are both confident.

My precious little boy is more like me. He is five years old, and I don't know how he has so much energy every day. He runs and falls everywhere – I try to cover up the hardwood in the house, but it doesn't help – and sometimes outside, he screams so loud that the birds fly away and then he cries. Poor guy. He is like his father in that he is so kind. I know in his tiny, innocent heart, that he is kind.

Just the other day, his little mind connected the dots. He said to me:

"Mama! If Uncle Devek (as he calls my brother) only had thirteen years left to live when he had his first baby, then won't he die in seven years if the baby is six now?"

It was going to click sooner or later, I guess. Better sooner. Then my baby boy can start to learn to appreciate each day.

The problem with the Waterkeepers before the Prophecies were fulfilled was that they were alone. They weren't happy or free. They served everyone in the world but themselves.

Since then, the world hasn't changed enough to grant the Keepers total freedom, to let them live with the people as they once did. It's changed just enough though. They are not in isolation – they can live with their families and go out into the world from time to time. They have happiness now.

I have happiness now.

But just because I live in Paradise, doesn't mean my life is one. Things have a way of catching up with you whether you're a servant of Luna or not. My mother died not too long ago; at least she never saw my Grief Cry. Whenever there is a drought or flood somewhere, a lot of pressure is put on the family too. And everyone has their off days. On those days, filled with sadness and frustration, when I think things couldn't get any worse, I go out to the waterfall. I sit there and look up at its majesty and listen to its constant, unending song, and I think about just how much worse it was when I didn't know what lay beyond the waterfall.